After the End

A Post Apocalyptic Adventure

Kevin Partner

SCRIBBLEIT
PUBLISHING

Scribbleit

CONTENTS

Introduction   V

1. Bane   1

2. Exciser   11

3. Deviant   18

4. Mecklen   25

5. McGinty's   33

6. Escape   40

7. Boston   46

8. Hiding   54

9. Marshes   61

10. Glass   69

11. Cardenas   75

12. Venkateshwara   84

13. Hannah   92

14. The Tower   99

15. The Swamplands   106

16. Burrell   113

17. Keller   120

18. New Haven   129

19. Xavier   134

20. Alone   141

21. Blossom   148

22. Skeeter   154

23. Roberto   160

24. The Tower   167

25. Marshes   173

26. Nadia   179

27. Fawn   186

28. Foundation   192

29. Glass   200

30. Eve   207

31. Floyd   213

Epilogue   220

Author's note   227

INTRODUCTION

2057, North America

Civilization is fragile; a house of cards built up over centuries, blown away in a moment.

What would happen if humanity was brought to the brink of extinction overnight? How would those who emerged from the rubble survive the next, desperate months?

That story is told in the *Nightfall* series.

This is the account of what happened later.

Thirty-five years later. This America is recognizable enough to those who'd lived through the apocalypse to be a constant reminder of what they'd lost. Relics of the past rot and crumble as the next generations forget their original purpose, and a mythology begins to develop, born of misunderstanding, disbelief and legends passed down from the few survivors of the old world.

This is a story of rebuilding from the ashes of the past. It would be a sore enough test if mankind only had to contend with the twisted and stunted remains of the world's ecology, almost obliterated by the twin radiation storms three and a half decades ago.

But evil flourishes in the ashes when power is wielded by those few who have control over the lives of others. The greatest enemy of humanity is itself.

And where there is evil, heroes will rise to oppose it.

The trick is being able to tell one from the other. The good from the bad, the hero from the villain.

Which of these is Reuben Bane?

Don't ask him.

He doesn't know himself.

But he's about to find out.

1

BANE

REUBEN BANE SAT WITH his back to a tree and stared into the embers, their gentle crackle like distant gunfire. Gently, he lowered the ancient, battered, priceless e-reader and focused his attention on the blackness beyond the little clearing.

Fools! Didn't he have enough blood on his hands already? Every death, whether deserved or not, took a piece of his soul with it, so that he wondered whether there was anything left of the man he had once been. The good man.

All he wanted was to get to Jackson in one piece, pick up some supplies and continue his journey leaving as little evidence of his passing through as possible. After all, he had hunters on his trail.

But rather than getting some much-needed sleep, he would have to deal with the rank amateurs hiding in the trees, waiting for their leader to spring the trap. He must have looked like easy pickings, a man travelling with no company but his big, black gelding.

Smart bandits would have stopped to think whether this truly was a lucky chance or whether he was alone because he didn't need the protection of numbers. But the collective intelligence of a group like this was never greater than that of its leader, and this one was about to make a fatal mistake.

Reuben wrapped the blanket around himself and noiselessly drew back the hammer of the revolver in his left hand, before repeating the action with its twin in his right.

He didn't stir as a large shape emerged into the dim red light of the dying fire.

"Don't move, mister," the man said, pointing the business end of a shotgun at Bane.

Reuben's eyes swiveled up from beneath his wide-brimmed hat. "I'm not moving. Now, why don't you put the gun down and sit by the fire? You're welcome to share what's left of my supplies."

"Oh, am I, though? That's mighty generous. Considering I could just take it for myself and not share it with no one."

He was trying to sound confident. A performance for the men hidden in the trees.

"What is your name, friend?"

"Crow, and I ain't your friend."

"Well, Mr. Crow, my name is Reuben Bane and I'm going to do you a kind deed. Go back the way you came and trouble me no more and you will live."

The big man roared with laughter. It was a good act, but an act nonetheless. "Seems to me you got this all kinds of wrong. I'm the one with the shotgun. And you clearly ain't noticed that my boys have got you surrounded."

"On the contrary, Mr. Crow. I know exactly where each of your three, no four, men are." Bane made a show of looking around the clearing as if his eyes could penetrate both darkness and trees.

Crow blinked in obvious surprise, but then recovered. "Then you know you ain't got no chance. Make a wrong move and my boys will open fire."

"Maybe, but that won't help you."

"Why?"

"Because you'll be dead."

At that, Crow's gun rose, and the silence exploded with an ear-shattering boom.

The bandit leader froze, looked down at his chest and folded up, hitting the ground as the echo disappeared.

There was a moment's silence.

Then, splinters spat from the tree behind where Bane had been sitting a moment before. He brought his arm up, rolling onto his side and sending a volley into the trees. Someone yelled and fell forward, half emerging from within the branches.

Reuben crouched in the shelter of the tree and called out, "Any of you feel like living through the night, you take your friends and go. I'll give you ten seconds to show yourself."

He tensed as he counted down, eyes scanning the gloom beyond the embers. Five to one they'd have the sense to do what he said, but he wasn't about to rely on those odds. He'd learned over the years never to underestimate sheer dumb stupidity.

As it happened, he only got to seven before a man emerged, hands held high, two other shapes lurking behind him,

"That all of you?"

"Yessir," the first man said. He was young and good-looking, and Reuben guessed it was he who'd made the decision to quit.

"What's your name, son?" Bane said, keeping his revolver trained on the speaker.

"Shawn Hill, sir. And this here's Tyler and Lennie James."

Reuben nodded and tilted his hat back. "I'm Reuben Bane. You won't forget that, will you?"

"No, sir. But ... but ... your face. You got the plague!"

Bane ran his hand along his jawline, feeling the rough pock-marks left by a disease that had taken his wife and child, but not him. Though he wished with all his heart it had.

"Not anymore, I haven't. Now, drop your weapons and drag your friends away. Bury them down the slope a little."

Hill looked at the two shapes on the ground and nodded.

"What the hell is wrong with you, Shawnie?" one of the two men behind said, grabbing Hill by the shoulder and pointing down at the body of the second man to die. "He just killed Del. What kind of friends are we if we don't do nothing about it?"

Bane got to his feet, sliding one of the two revolvers back into its holster. "You'll be the living kind."

"But he had a wife and a kid!"

"So did I, once," Reuben said as he began to feel the adrenaline tide go out and the darkness gather. "Look, I'm sorry for your friend, but most men don't get even one chance to take a shot at me. I will help you give him a decent burial."

He took a stride toward the fallen man, but Shawn put his hand out. "No, we'll handle it. Lennie's right, we owe it to his wife."

"And the man you followed?" Bane said, gesturing at the corpse of their leader.

"Leave him lie."

Reuben rubbed his back as he stood by the grave-side. He'd dug a hole for Crow helped by the third of the gang, the twin of the argumentative Lennie. Tyler, however, had dug in silence as his brother and Shawn made a grave for their friend, working in the light of Reuben's oil lamp.

Together, he and Tyler then dragged the body into the trench, then helped to carry their friend to his final resting place. Bane was in the blackest of moods by the time they began filling it back in.

"Anyone know any words?" Shawn said when they'd finished.

Reuben sagged as he felt their eyes on him and, with a sigh, spoke. "'The Lord is my shepherd; I shall not want. He maketh me to lie down in green pastures: he leadeth me beside the still waters.'"

When he'd finished, Shawn turned to him. "You said that from memory?"

"I have buried many," Bane said. "Now, I will go on my way. Do not follow."

"But it's after midnight. You shouldn't be travelling in the dark."

"Why? In case I come across bandits like you? I can handle myself."

Shawn shook his head as they walked back up the slope toward where Bane's horse waited patiently. "We were wrong, I'm sorry."

"Is this the part where you claim it was all Crow's fault? He led you astray, did he?"

Reuben swung around to look at the young man who hesitated for a moment before shaking his head. "No. We followed him willing."

Good, the boy had some integrity.

"You're not a fool, Shawn, but you know this kind of life only ends one way. Why?"

"Come back to our camp and let us feed you, will you? It's late to be riding tonight and we're not the only ..."

"Bandits? Brigands?"

"Yeah. There's more out there. You'll be safe with us."

Reuben examined the young man's face, but saw no deception. And, after so many years as an exciser, he knew a lie when he saw one.

"What about Lennie?"

"He'll be okay. Del was a pal of his, but he knows you had no choice."

"Oh, I had a choice alright, but I can't die yet. I've got one last task to accomplish before I can rest in peace."

Reuben sat beside the fire and ate his beans as the twins pointedly ignored him.

"Good beans?" Shawn said, putting the ladle back in the little cauldron and settling down beside him.

Reuben nodded. "They are, thank you."

"My mom makes them. Says they're almost as good as the ones in the old times." He looked sideways in Bane's direction, raising an eyebrow.

"Almost. And yes, I'm old enough to remember when beans came in a can."

"I heard tell that a factory over in Pittsburgh makes them that way."

"Sure."

"You think one day everything will be back like it was? Everything in cans? Then we could have apples all year round. And meat that keeps forever."

Reuben smiled. Humanity had fallen so low that this was the limit of a young man's vision. From Shawn's perspective, canning promised the end of the cycle of feast and famine that had plagued his life. It had been so long since the collapse of mankind that even Reuben craved the most basic technological recovery, and canned meat would be a major advance on how things were right now. But he also remembered a time of conspicuous plenty when he hadn't given a thought to where what he ate came from or when his next meal would be.

"Mom's got a collection of jars. Don't tell no one, they're worth a fortune. She cooks this catchup and seals it. Most of it, she sells, but she gave me a jar to come away with, and a bag of dried beans."

"Does she know you're a brigand?"

Shawn reddened and shook his head. "No. Crow came into the village and said he was lookin' for help on his farm. Said it was down Raymond way, but we hadn't been gone for more than a couple of days when he said he knew an easier way of makin' money for thems who was willin' to bend the rules. Del, he was dead set against it, but me and the twins, we couldn't go back empty-handed. None of us has got two cents to rub together and the blight knocked us for six. Besides, Crow said we was just going to ambush a tax wagon and take back what was owed us."

The words were tumbling out now, so Reuben stayed quiet while the young man spoke.

"And we did it. We took out the tax wagon, but it was ... it was ... not what I thought. They were only folks like us, grateful to have a job. But we killed them all. I was so scared, Mr. Bane. I don't know what came over me, but I did my share of the killing. And then we figured we couldn't go back anyways, not until the fuss had died down."

Shawn subsided, breathing out a lungful of air as if unburdened.

"How long ago was this?"

"A month."

"And how many others have you ambushed? Before you tried to do the same to me?"

"Five or six. But most folks gave up when Crow told 'em to."

"Most?"

He nodded; eyes cast down. "Ma will never forgive me. She thinks I'm making an honest wage. But if I hadn't gone with Crow, we'd have all starved come winter."

"It's only the spring, plenty of time to plant and harvest."

"You gotta have something to plant. We got the blight, lost most of the crop and had to sell what was left. We only saved a little, and most of that got the weevil. Government's quick enough to take our taxes, not so fast to help us out when we need it."

Reuben finished his beans and put the pan down. "Government was never much good at that. Just be grateful the Foundation doesn't rule here."

"I heard their people never starve."

Bane chuckled mirthlessly. "Depends on who you mean by their people. There are plenty of fat brothers in Boston, but a hundred times more starving unsaved toiling in the fields to feed them."

"It's hard to believe nobody starved back in the old times."

"Oh, plenty did. Especially in other countries. Now the whole world shares the misery. So, I guess, in a twisted kind of way, that's progress."

He got to his feet and washed his pan in a small stream on the other side of the camp before returning to the fire and holding out his hand to Shawn. "It'll be dawn soon enough and I have to get moving, but thanks for your hospitality."

Shawn stood and shook. "Thanks for not killing us. I think you could have shot us all without much trouble."

"I'm glad. I have enough blood on me as it is. And I'll give you some advice before I go." He walked to where the black gelding waited before climbing into the saddle with a groan of effort.

"I'll be glad to hear it," Shawn said.

Reuben looked down at him, then at the twins, glowering in the firelight. "You're not fools, so stop acting like you are. Go home and find a way to make an honest living."

One of the twins got to his feet. "You want us to tell them we ambushed the wagon?"

"A lie of omission. Just say you've been sent home from Crow's farm and know nothing about the ambush."

Shawn sighed. "Even if they don't string us up for that, we'll die with all the others when winter comes."

"Then you'll die honest," Reuben said, marveling at his own hypocrisy. "That is my advice, but you're under no obligation to do as I say. It's up to you to make your choice."

He nudged the horse away and, with a final farewell, guided the beast through the trees and back onto the highway.

Ten minutes later, he heard the faint echo of a gunshot, and his heart sank. "I guess someone's made their choice," he said to himself.

2

EXCISER

RUEBEN SWUNG HIS LEG over the horse's back and dropped from the saddle. He didn't look up at the dead. He knew they were there. He'd seen them as he approached the ruined town. Their ropes groaned in the breeze even as warning bells pealed on the other side of the wall.

"Welcome to Jackson," he muttered, stroking Lucifer's face before leading him toward the gate. His exposure patch glowed purple in his other hand. Time to get under cover.

He'd planned to pass by the town, to keep ahead of the hunters who pursued him, but then the cursed lights had appeared for the first time in months, and he'd been forced to scuttle for cover like a cockroach. It had been either that or a night sharing his travel cloak with the horse in some ruin on the outskirts. He'd spent all day brooding over his encounter with Shawn and the others twenty miles west of here and found, for once, he craved company and a real bed for a night.

A man wearing an antique Army helmet emerged from the sentry hut, pistol in one hand, oil lamp in the other. "Town's closed, stranger."

"I seek shelter." Reuben gestured up at the dancing bands of rainbow light in the night sky.

"Like I said. Town's closed." The guard had a straggly beard and the brittle confidence of youth.

Rueben sighed. "Law says you gotta provide shelter for travelers."

"I got my orders. No one's allowed in on account of the plague. Not without examination."

"So, examine me," Reuben said, stepping forward into the yellow light of the lamp, exposing his scarred face.

The revolver muzzle jerked away. "Get back! You got it!"

"I *had* it. I ain't gonna get it again. Now, you have a choice, son. You can either let me in, or you can find someone who'll make that call because, one way or another, I'm gonna shelter here tonight."

The guard called over his shoulder. "Merle!"

"What's goin' on out here?" The business end of a double barrelled shotgun appeared in the air beside the guard.

"Stranger says we gotta give him shelter. Says it's the law."

"You tell him about the plague, boy?"

"Says he's —"

"I've already had it," Reuben spat, his patience at an end. He took off his hat and threw back his hood, exposing the faded scars and pockmarks lining his jaw and throat. "The sickness took my wife and daughter and I wish to Almighty God it had taken me but, it seems he's not finished with me yet."

The second man nodded, rubbing his chin as if to check his own face. "You know, you should take care with your words, stranger. Some folks would call that blasphemy."

He edged a little closer, examining Reuben's face, his lip curling as the lantern made the scars even more obvious. "Yeah, all healed up. But we ain't got room, and the law's the law. You should hunker down out here somewhere and take the examination tomorrow."

With the speed of a striking rattlesnake, Reuben grabbed the gun barrel, wrenching it out of the guard's grip, then dropped it as he drew his Colt 1911. The two guards froze like statues.

Then he smiled and holstered his weapon.

"What the hell?" the older guard said, raising his eyebrow. "Put the gun down, boy," he added to the youth behind him.

"You'll let me in?"

Merle shrugged and shook his head. "We got our orders."

Grabbing hold of the cuff of his travel-stained canvas jacket, Reuben put the older guard between him and the other. Then he rolled his sleeve up.

Merle's jaw dropped as he gasped. "But ... but ... That's the mark of ..."

Reuben lifted a finger to his lips and the older guard went silent, before stepping back, hushing the younger man's questions.

"Am I free to proceed?"

"Of course, master." Merle made a waving gesture.

"Where could I find lodging for myself and my horse?"

Merle, whose demeanor had spun on its axis, made a show of considering that. "Well, you could try McGinty's, Ox has usually got space, though the town's bursting at the seams. Shall I send a runner to find out?"

"No, thank you. I'll find somewhere," Reuben said, leading the horse past the barrier and into the town. Damn the man's intransigence. He'd hoped to slip in and out of the town without causing any disturbance, but this man would remember him and the markings on the underside of his forearm. He had to hope that it was long before others came here, pursuing him.

For the thousandth time he wished with all his heart he'd never become an exciser. No profession was loathed as much, no men so hated as those who identified and terminated deviants.

And no man was more earnestly hunted than he who turns his back on the holy order. For Reuben Bane, there was nowhere safe to hide.

For now, however, he led his horse quickly through Jackson's deserted street. He'd covered the beast's flank with his silvered cloak, but had nothing more substantial than a reinforced hood to protect his brain from cooking under the aurora's malevolent glare.

He felt eyes watching him from the shadows as he passed like a ghost accompanied only by the gentle *clip-clop* of hooves on asphalt. Keeping one hand on the bridle, the other on his 1911, he kept his head still while his eyes scanned a darkness relieved only by the orange flames of the street braziers.

Reuben fought back a yawn, pushing away the exhaustion of a fortnight in the wilderness — this would not be a good time to show any signs of weakness. There was no better time to attack a stranger than when everyone was supposed to be taking shelter. Anyone who tried it with him wouldn't have time to learn from their mistake, but there was always the risk of injury and, most importantly, drawing attention to himself.

He saw McGinty's by the light leaking from behind its shuttered windows before he could make out the sign above the door. What had once been a motel was now the main drinking establishment of a much smaller Jackson, that clung to the skirts of a mummified city.

A man emerged into the night, silhouetted against the orange glow of the tavern's interior. He stood, ax in hand gesturing Reuben to wait.

"I don't recognize you," the man said.

"Name's Reuben Bane. You Ox?"

"John Oxendine. You know me?"

Reuben nodded in the direction of the south gate. "I was told you might have lodging for me and my horse."

Oxendine's eyes switched to the animal. "Looks a fine beast."

"Should have been put out to pasture years ago but, you know."

The innkeeper nodded, the hand on his ax relaxing a little. Horses were worth more than silver and, in general, ridden until they dropped. "What's your business?"

"Just passing through. Do you have room for me? I can pay."

"Ammo? Smokes?"

"Silver." Reuben reached into his inside pocket and held out a sliver of metal that glittered in the darkness.

Oxendine's eye's flashed as he moved quickly forward. Reuben could have easily taken him out as he did so, ax or no ax, but then he'd have the townsfolk on his heels as he tried to escape. And the man was harmless in his judgement.

"It'll cost you three ounces."

Reuben held the innkeeper's gaze. Both men knew the price was three times the going rate for a night's lodging, even including stabling.

"I'll take two," Oxendine said after a few seconds of silence.

Reuben dropped the three slivers into Oxendine's meaty hand. "Three is fine, Mr. Oxendine."

"Call me Ox," he said, then turned back to where a figure waited beside the door. "Go fetch Seamus and tell him he's got to find room and fresh hay for Mr. Reuben's beast."

The figure disappeared inside; the hubbub quickly truncated as the door closed behind him.

Reuben waited just long enough for the silence to become awkward before saying, "What's the news? Guard at the gate says there's plague around."

"Yeah. That's why I was surprised to see you. Orders are no one's allowed in after dark. Harder to examine folks without daylight."

Reuben nodded. "I don't need much examination. Had the plague a year ago, won't get it again."

The innkeeper went to step backward then caught himself and planted his foot down before mumbling an apology.

"Nothing wrong with being frightened of the plague," Reuben said. "But tell me, who runs Jackson these days? Last I heard you had a city council."

Oxendine lowered his voice. "Best we go inside. Loose talk and all."

At that moment, the hostler appeared and took the horse's reins.

"Now, you look after Mr. Bane's beast, Seamus, you hear me?"

"Yes, Mr. Oxendine," the young man said, his black ponytail jumping up and down as he nodded. "He's a fine horse, sir," he added to Reuben as he took the reins. "What do I call him?"

"Lucifer's his name, on account of his temperament when he was young."

Reuben watched as the young hostler led Lucifer, smiling at the way he kept the horse at arm's length as if he might turn into his namesake at any moment.

3

DEVIANT

REUBEN SAT AT A table and sipped at his drink, eyes taking in the bar. It had been six months since he'd last been in such a crowded space, and, within minutes, he found himself craving the relative quiet of his room. When he'd first come down, the volume had dropped as the assembled company evaluated him, and there'd been a collective gasp when he'd sat at a table and the candlelight had made his scars obvious. In fact, Reuben suspected the innkeeper had prepared the company because, had he not, many people would have left, fearing disease more than the lights in the sky.

But, after the initial shock, conversation resumed and he now found himself largely ignored, which was how he liked it. His ears adjusted more quickly than his nose, which found itself assaulted by the complex miasma of many people in a small space drinking and eating.

He swallowed another mouthful, leaned back and sighed. An acceptable brew, though, as always, more malty than hoppy. It had been a long decade between the end of the world and the first barley crops with enough surplus to allow for malting but, boy, what would he give for a cold IPA?

His thoughts were interrupted as the food arrived and he nodded at the girl even as she placed the plate on the table at arm's length alongside a fresh pint before scampering quickly away.

The meat was a lump of salted pig masquerading as gammon, but it probably represented the best the tavern could offer, and was tasty enough. Having spent months surviving on charity, dried jerky and the occasional scrawny rabbit, it was a relief to fill his stomach, even if there was more fat than meat and some of it tougher than his leather coat. He pushed the plate away and finally felt himself relax. Truth was, nowhere was entirely safe for anyone, let alone a hunted former exciser, but a full belly and decent beer somehow made the danger recede a little.

Then he noticed Oxendine hovering at the bar and looking in his direction. Suppressing the temptation to roll his eyes or ignore the man, he waved him over.

"I'm sorry to disturb your meal, Mr. Bane, but it's just that, well, I just wanted to make sure we'd given satisfaction."

Rueben sighed. "You've obviously heard then. Yes, I'm an exciser," he said. "Do you wish to see my mark?"

"Oh, no. No, indeed, your lordship."

"I'm no lord, believe me. And yes, the meal was excellent, as is the beer."

Oxendine seemed to deflate as if he'd been holding his breath. "I sure am pleased to hear that. But I wonder if I could ask a favor."

"Go ahead."

The innkeeper leaned forward and lowered his voice. "Well, you see, sir, it's like this. We haven't had a visit in such a while, and there's a matter that can only be settled by a man such as yourself."

Rueben nodded, his heart sinking as he sensed a trap opening up in front of him.

"We got one, you see," Oxendine continued. "A deviant. In the basement. We're holding him for the next official visit, but who knows when that will be?"

"When was the last?"

"Six months ago, at least."

Rueben felt the tension in his body ease. It seemed the Foundation wasn't especially interested in Jackson. Hopefully that applied to their hunters as much as their regular excisers. He needed to get out of town without raising suspicion, and the best way to do that was to play along with Oxendine.

He just hoped the man was wrong.

Rueben's heart sank as he reached the bottom of the basement stairs and caught sight of the deviant.

"He's just a boy," he said, looking back at the inn-keeper's nervous face in the lantern-light.

Oxendine shrugged. "It sure is a shame. And he looks normal. I guess that's how he's gotten away with it."

"What's the story?"

"His parents tried to sneak him in. They sure must have been desperate to think they'd get past the examiner. Tried to bribe him, or so it's said."

Rueben shook his head. "Where are they now?" He knew the answer, but he needed the man to say the words.

The innkeeper looked back up the stairs as if he couldn't wait to escape. His voice dropped to a whisper. "Hanging from the gate gallows."

Bane saw the two bodies in his memory, creaking on the end of their ropes.

"Law's clear enough on that," Oxendine continued, "but the boy's committed no crime. If it was up to me ..."

"What?"

Oxendine's face drained of all color, and he froze as he tried to form a sequence of words that wouldn't see him join the boy's parents hanging on the end of a rope.

Reuben put the man out of his misery. "Fortunately, it is not up to you, Oxendine. It is the role of excisers to make these decisions in accordance with scripture and Foundation teachings. Now, you will leave me to examine the boy."

The innkeeper didn't wait for Rueben to repeat the order, but scampered up the basement steps at a remarkable pace considering his size, and disappeared. Bane waited until he heard the door close, and approached the boy who, it turned out, was chained to a slave ring on the floor.

"What is your name?" he said, getting onto his haunches and examining the child with his eyes. Twelve or thirteen years of age, Rueben guessed, and bone-thin, he shrank away with his knees under his chin as if they could shield him from the exciser. "We don't have time for this. You will tell me your name, willing or no."

For the first time, the boy looked directly at him. "Asha. My name's Asha."

His voice was barely above a whisper, and he trembled as he spoke.

"And your family name?"

"They call me Ash."

"No, I mean your surname. The name your family shares."

The boy shook his head, clearly not understanding what Reuben was saying.

"Where did you live before you came here?"

"Home."

Reuben sighed, rocking back on his haunches then settling on the dusty concrete floor. He knew the story. Mother had the child, discovered he was a mutant and then she and the father kept him away from what passed for civilization, so he had a chance to grow up without coming under examination. But something changed and they were forced to try and slip in. His blemish must have been a minor one or they wouldn't have tried, however desperate.

And the boy clearly hadn't heard of the excisers, or he'd be much more terrified than he actually was. Or perhaps he simply hadn't recognized one when he was sitting in front of him.

"I need to examine you," Reuben said. "It would help if you could explain to me what makes you different to your parents."

At their mention, he screwed up his face and the tears came, the basement echoing with anguished sobs.

This was not in Reuben's wheelhouse. He half leaned forward, feeling as though there was something he should do to comfort the boy, but, in the end, slumped back and waited, eyes searching for any signs of deformity.

All he could see, however, was that the child was as thin as a wraith, the line of his shoulder-blades obvious as he sat, curled up and heaved.

"I'm sorry, Asha, but if I am to protect you, then you must tell me how you're different."

The tears subsided and the boy's voice emerged from somewhere within his curled-up form. "I know what people are thinking."

"What? You can read minds? No, of course not." Reuben knew this was simply a child's fantasy. After all, why would his parents feel the need to hide him in that case? "There is something on your body that is different. I must know, Asha. You can trust me." He wondered, as he said those final four words, how often they'd been abused, and he felt sick to his stomach.

"I know. That man who came with you, he was frightened. He felt sorry for me. But you won't hurt me. You're very sad."

Reuben ground his teeth. The last thing he needed was to be psychoanalyzed by a kid. For an instant he wondered what had happened to the psychiatrists after the end of the world. He saw, in his mind's eye, a comfortable couch in a sunny room. A woman was taking notes.

It was another world, lost in time, never to be recovered.

"Asha, we have no time. You must tell me, now. Do you have extra toes?" It cut him to the core to ask, but he was all out of time. In his memory, he saw a baby's hand and the tiny extra finger that condemned it.

The boy looked up at him, as if he finally understood. "No," he said, but then he slipped off his leather sandals.

At first, Reuben could see nothing unusual. Thank God, there were five toes on each foot.

Then Asha took his big toe in one hand and the smallest digit in another and separated them.

"You have webs." Reuben said, hopelessly.

4

MECKLEN

DOCTOR HANNAH MYERS WATCHED as the man shuffled into the courtroom, his ankle chains sliding over the polished wood floor. She could see from his defeated expression that he knew as well as she did that this was only going to end one way.

But Mayor Mitchell Snider sure liked to put on a show. One of his many mantras was that if justice wasn't served publicly then it wasn't justice at all.

Snider leaned back in the center chair and looked down at the prisoner in the dock.

"The defendant will state his name for the court to hear."

"You know me, Mitch. Known me all your life. Heck, everyone in this courtroom knows me." He gestured around at the small crowd of onlookers, though most of them didn't react.

Hannah glanced to her right to see Snider tense with obvious irritation.

"This is not a social occasion. Please respect the court's procedures and state your name."

"Gene Burrell," the man said with a sigh.

Hannah knew him, of course. In his mid-sixties, he had grown up in the old world, as she had, but he'd made a new life after the twin extinction events almost wiped out humanity. Almost? They'd probably achieve it in the end, but with a slow, lingering death rather than the killing blow she'd feared when she'd detected the second radiation storm all those years ago.

When she'd fled from her past, headed east and ended up settling in Mecklen, Gene Burrell had been here. At the time, he farmed land on the banks of the Potomac River, and, by the standards of this new world, he was comfortably off, selling his surplus grain in the market here and in Martinsburg. But then, two years ago, his crop had been swept away in the great storm along with all his stores. He was a thinner, disheveled shadow of the man he'd once been.

"Mr. Burrell," Snider continued in the clipped voice he reserved for official occasions, "you are accused of multiple counts of theft. The clerk will read out the list of indictments."

Hannah tried to keep her expression neutral as she listened. She'd never wanted to be on the council, but Snider's predecessor had insisted on it as a condition of her becoming a permanent citizen of the town. And it was just her luck that this man's case had come up when it had been her turn to sit as one of the three members of the judicial panel.

She'd been a scientist once. Perhaps she still was, though she now worked alone, and it had been her community of colleagues that had, in her view, defined what she did as science. That community had been eliminated in one night thirty-five years ago, but she'd found a smaller and even more precious group in the months before the second wave hit. They'd lost one member to the violence of those times, but had emerged to at least some hope.

And, in many ways, that hope had been justified. New Haven had flourished — as far as it's possible to flourish in the arid environment of North Nevada as the world got drier and drier. On a personal level, however, it didn't work out and, once she'd done what she'd agreed to do, she headed east and ended up here in West Virginia.

Snider's voice snapped her out of brooding on the past. "How do you plead?"

Rather than answer, Burrell turned to face the spectators. "I've wronged some of you here, and I can't apologize enough. I stole from you, Maisie, and I didn't step forward when you were accusing others. And you, Chester. I shouldn't have done it, I know that."

A middle-aged woman stood up and looked directly at Burrell. "I forgave you long ago, Gene. You were generous when you had plenty, and we should have looked out for you when you lost it all."

"Mr. Burrell," Snider said, the pitch and volume of his voice betraying his irritation. "How do you plead?"

Gene Burrell turned to face the three judges, glancing at Hannah last before she could drop her gaze.

"I am guilty of those charges," he said. "But you know my family was starving, Mitchell."

"Many starved after the flood, Mr. Burrell. Not all of them stole from their neighbors. Not even after the blight came last year."

Burrell shook his head. "You know why — I have people I was responsible for who weren't counted for food distribution. I had five ration cards and fifteen folk to feed."

"Then you should have kept your farm worker registrations up to date. Or sent them away when the crop was washed out."

"Retrospect is a fine thing, ain't it? Not all of us can look back at the past and know we got every last decision we made right."

Snider's face visibly tightened. "Let it be entered into the record that the defendant pled guilty to all charges. Now, the court will retire to consider its verdict. Court is suspended."

The words had barely left Snider's lips when he stood, pushing his ornate chair back with a judder that echoed around the courtroom, and he headed for the judges' chambers.

Hannah waited at the door of the chambers for the court to empty, before following Snider inside.

"Come in, Doctor," the mayor said, gesturing at a chair. "This shouldn't take long."

Hannah shook her head. "I've been sitting for long enough today, thank you."

Snider shrugged and leaned back, the leather-padding of the seat cushion creaking beneath him, then he turned his attention to the third judge. She was a diminutive woman who sat on the other side of the huge desk, her face illuminated by the light from an oil lantern.

"Mrs. Beal, do you have an opinion on what we've just seen?"

"Oh, please call me Ida, Mitch. You know I can't abide formality."

"We're in a courthouse. If we're not formal here, where would we be?"

"But the door's shut and all."

Snider held her gaze for a moment as if he could put the 'fluence on her. Then, when she showed no sign of bending to his will, he sighed. "Very well, Ida. Now, will you favor us with your opinion?"

The older woman shifted in her chair, then leaned forward. "Well, it's like this. I've known Gene Burrell for more than forty years and he's no more a thief than I am."

"And yet he stole food. He admitted as much."

"Because the town didn't help him enough after the flood."

"The town had its own problems."

"Sure enough, but it seems to me we could show a little mercy to a man who has this town's name written on his heart."

Snider made a moaning noise. "None of that alters the fact that he stole from his neighbors. You just heard him confess in open court."

"And I heard him making peace with those very neighbors. I dare say he's done the same with the others he wronged. Maybe we should ask *them* what should happen to him."

"Mob rule, you mean?" Snider snapped. "Thieves get let off if they're popular? No, not in my town. How many other places do you know where the rule of law is maintained as it was before the fall?"

Both Hannah and Ida Beale had been adults when the auroras had first appeared, whereas Mitch Snider was born in the first years afterward. Perhaps he'd manipulated the court roster to make sure his fellow judges were old enough to remember the old world.

The truth was, Hannah knew of only one other town where she'd be confident to walk the streets at night, and that was fifteen hundred miles away in the Nevada desert. And she hadn't always agreed with the decisions its mayor had made, either. She wasn't so naive as to think that it was easy to maintain order, and if she were to be fair to Snider, the town was generally at peace.

But he was a sneaky son of a bitch, and she was pretty certain he had an angle on this that she hadn't spotted yet.

Maybe it was nothing more than putting one of the other main figures in town life out of the picture so he could continue to dominate. Though, in truth, Burrell had faded into the background after the Potomac flooded. There were still parts of the city that were buried under tons of mud. More people now lived in houses built since the fall than in the more sophisticated dwellings that survived. Like this court room.

Just as the river had been the town's downfall, it was also its salvation. The mud it had deposited over the centuries had formed the perfect clay for making bricks, and Mecklen was now the source of most of the building material for the surrounding towns. Its bricks were even being used by the so-called Federal government to rebuild DC.

So, bricks flowed out of Mecklen and paid for the food to flow back in again.

And Mayor Mitchell Snider owned the brickworks.

"Look," he said, softening his voice. "I understand this is a difficult matter, but that's why we're here, as leaders of the community. To make the tough decisions. Without law and justice, how long do you think we'd survive? You remember what happened in Charles Town? Have you forgotten the poor harvest last year? Starving people need firm government if we're not to have open rebellion."

Then he turned his attention on Hannah. "What do you think, Doctor?"

She sighed as she slumped into the chair beside Ida. "I take your point. People must know that we have the rule of law here or there'll be anarchy. But there's sometimes a difference between law and justice. This is one of those occasions."

"That's right, darlin'," Ida said. "And your cute British accent is just the cherry on the pie."

Mitch Snider looked from one to the other, tugging at his ear. Hannah could tell he was nervous and frustrated. Maybe he'd hoped she'd pull the answer out of thin air, but this was a much more difficult puzzle to solve than the many discussions they'd had about agriculture yield and population levels over the years.

"Trouble is, Mr. Mayor," Hannah said, "whichever thread we choose to pull could make the whole jumper fall apart, but we won't know until we pull it. If we find him guilty, then we don't have much leeway, whether we follow the Foundation mandate or our local laws, and hanging a man like him is going to cause resentment at best, and maybe revolt. Can Sheriff Mendez handle it, do you think? Are all his men loyal?"

Snider sprang to his feet, frustration obvious. "And if we let him off, then we can give up any pretense that we operate under the rule of law. He's a self-confessed thief."

"Well, Mr. Mayor," Ida said, shaking her head, "seems to me we're in a fix. As chairman of this here panel, I guess it's gonna be up to you."

Hannah watched Snider's face. This wasn't what he'd become mayor and chief justice for. He'd never made a decision in his life that he couldn't blame someone else for if it backfired. She found herself wondering how he'd get out of this one.

"Doctor Myers, you're the most educated among us —"

"I'm an astrophysicist, not a lawyer!"

"— so figure it out. You've got forty-eight hours."

So, there it was. Now the fate of Gene Burrell and, perhaps, the entire town, rested on her shoulders.

5

McGinty's

REUBEN LAY IN BED, unable to get the boy's face out of his mind. It wasn't the obvious fear as he'd looked up at his captor, trying to read his expression, it was his confusion. The boy wondered why would it matter that he had flaps of skin between his toes that linked them together?

Why, indeed?

This was uncomfortable terrain for Reuben Bane, a man who'd spent three decades believing that the only way for the human species to survive was to rid the gene pool of all contamination. He was no scientist, but he was old enough to remember the world before the first aurora and he understood something of the effect radiation had on the rate of mutation.

Of course, the Foundation had corrupted this into a doctrine of purity and, to his shame, Reuben Bane had bought into it so completely that he'd trained as an exciser, hunting and eliminating those discovered with mutations.

Eliminating?

Murdering.

And then, when he'd finally escaped into retirement, he'd found that the universe had a twisted sense of humor.

He'd lost so much because he'd chosen this path. Back in the old world, he'd been another person entirely. He'd even had another name. Then, he'd found a group of people to survive Armageddon with, sheltering underground as the second, deadliest wave hit. They'd emerged into a dead world, but he'd thought he could build some kind of a future with his new family. He was barely more than a boy himself, and had a child's optimism despite the leg wound he'd sustained in the last days of his subterranean existence. He still walked with a slight limp to this day; a constant reminder that he was once someone else.

But he'd left his new home after a few years, for reasons that made no sense to him now. And when he'd returned, it had gone, the people vanished into the dust. So, he'd sought a new family with the Foundation, and that had been the route to his damnation.

By any objective measure, he was the embodiment of evil.

But he couldn't let the boy in the basement die.

Truth was, there could be no permanent escape for Asha, no chance of a long-term future. But any future was better than none.

He had no plan beyond escaping this place and the city. He couldn't see beyond that, so it would have to do. He'd have to improvise. Perhaps the people in Haven — the ones who'd saved him from the plague — perhaps they'd take the boy in. But they were fifteen hundred miles away, a desert town in the middle of the Western wastelands, A region that had once been called Nevada.

Reuben lit the candle by his bed, then swung his feet onto the floor and crept to where his outer clothes lay on a chair, his hands working independently of his eyes as he dressed himself. Then he stood and listened, closing his eyes and breathing as quietly as possible. He heard the creaks and cracks of a building cooling in the middle night, and the occasional rumble of someone moving in their bed. The tavern only had half a dozen guestrooms, and he looked out of the window at the sky to see that the aurora had faded away. So, chances were the clientele had made their way home except, perhaps for the odd drunk who couldn't be bothered to move.

He slid his knife into its sheath in his belt and holstered the 1911. It was his proudest possession, but also a source of weakness because it made him reliant on armorers and that meant towns. So, he had a pair of cap and ball revolvers that he used day to day. Inferior weapons built in recent years, but reliable. Gunpowder and lead balls were much easier to come by than a .45 cartridge and much cheaper, even when he traded in his spent brass.

On the table beside the bed lay his straight sword which he usually wore on his back when riding and at his hip otherwise. He didn't like it much, but the training of an exciser involves becoming proficient with the blade and it was extremely effective at close quarters. But also much more cruel. A bullet in the head ended things much quicker than a slashing cut.

In a gunfight, the Colt was his best friend, giving him a massive edge over any modern weapon when it came to reliability, power and accuracy. Having said that, he couldn't shoot his way out of Jackson. His hope lay in silence and subtlety.

He opened the door of his room, wincing as it creaked on its rusty hinge, then crept out onto the landing, his pack on his back and weapons at his side, lantern held in front. Every few steps, he'd freeze, expecting to hear movement or even to be confronted by someone emerging from a bedroom. But he heard nothing are he snuck along the landing and down the stairs.

Drunken snoring cloaked the sounds of his footsteps as he made his cautious way downstairs. The place stank of stale alcohol, vomit and pure, bestial humanity and he couldn't wait to be outside in the fresh air again.

Finding the door to the basement, he was relieved that the innkeeper had left the key on the outside. That simplified things a little, but he knew, as he crept down the wooden stairs, that if the kid made any noise now, or he was discovered down here by a drunk wandering by the open door, he'd be cornered.

But the child seemed to be asleep. Reuben swung the lantern toward the curled-up form, and he felt his throat congeal in guilt and pity. No child should have to endure what this boy had suffered. And his future held more misery, as far as Reuben could see.

He got onto his haunches and put his hand over the boy's mouth. Instantly, the child tensed, arms flailing as he came around.

"Be quiet!" he hissed. "I'm not going to hurt you, but if you cry out, we'll both be dead by morning."

This seemed to sink in. The child gave a tiny nod and Rueben withdrew his hand slowly.

"What's happening?"

"These people will kill you, as they killed your parents. You understand this?"

The boy's eyes dropped to the filthy cement floor. Again, he nodded.

Reuben examined the padlock fastening the chain to the loop in the floor. It was primitive, but effective for most purposes. Not for keeping an exciser out, however. Sometimes, a good hunter of deviants is forced to resort to tricks the ignorant would consider magic.

The padlock dropped away, and the boy rubbed at his ankle. Reuben could see him struggling against the urge to make a run for the unlocked basement door. He saw him struggle and win. Good. Perhaps there was some hope for the boy, after all.

Reuben picked up the lantern, and held out his other hand to the child. "We must get to Lucifer, somehow."

"L ... Lucifer?" the boy gasped, wide-eyed.

"My horse."

"You're ... you're not ...?"

For the first time in a while, Reuben felt the skin at the corners of his mouth stretch into a smile. "No, I'm not the Devil." The grin disappeared as he wondered at how he could claim that. If a man is judged by his actions, then surely Reuben Bane deserved to be committed to the deepest dungeons of the underworld. Could he ever redeem himself? No, that was impossible. It was a question of setting an ounce of credit to the other side of the scales of judgment.

He guided the boy up the steps, ears straining for any sign of movement outside, then waited at the door, listening. But all he could hear was the thumping of his heart and Asha's frightened panting.

Drawing in a deep breath, he let Asha's hand go, extinguished the flame in the lantern, and drew his knife before gently opening the door.

The corridor outside was utterly silent.

Too silent.

Taking the boy's hand again, he crept out, keeping low and moving silently toward the parlor door.

Something was in here, breathing gently as if asleep. Something or someone.

Reuben guided Asha, taking a course as far from the sound of breathing as they could manage while taking care not to collide with anything. A shape emerged, the faint light coming in through the window picking out a darker shape among the darkness.

It was Oxendine.

A bottle of liquor lay by his side, the air seeped in the smell of rum. They wouldn't be able to get by without waking the man, and yet there was no other way out.

The simplest answer would be to cut the man's throat while he slept, but Reuben had abandoned the simple path when he'd turned his back on the past. He missed that sense of certainty, though he now knew it to be a fantasy; a certainty born of convenience. Life was so much easier when he'd known he was doing God's work as a defender of humanity. It took a long time to realized that he was, in fact, the opposite. A long time and a personal tragedy. He thought of his daughter, remembering that moment when she'd been revealed, swaddled against the cold, that moment of joy and relief ripped apart as her hand was revealed.

So, the simple answer was to kill Oxendine. He probably deserved it. He'd imprisoned the boy and, though he wouldn't have had a role in the deaths of the parents, he was prepared to deliver Asha to the excisers when they visited next. Was it reasonable to expect a man like this to put his life on the line to resist the law, even if he thought it unjust?

All that was irrelevant right now. Right now, the man was a problem.

Reuben maneuvered himself until he was behind the innkeeper then, in one movement, pressed his palm over Oxendine's mouth and held the knife up in front of his eyes.

Oxendine convulsed, arms flailing as he came around, then saw the metal shining in the reflected light from the windows and went still.

"Hold still, and you won't be harmed. Cry out and you die."

6

ESCAPE

REUBEN WITHDREW HIS HAND and allowed the innkeeper to twist around.

"I ... I don't understand ... master ..."

"That's not your place, Oxendine. All I require from you is to take me to your stables. We'll be away, you will go to your bed, and, in the morning, you'll discover we've gone. Understood?"

He watched as the inn-keeper's mind slowly digested what he was asking. Then Oxendine finally noticed Asha who was crouching behind the exciser, trembling.

Reuben grabbed the big man by the greasy collar of his shirt. "Do you understand?"

"But ... but master. The boy is ... is ..."

"The boy is a boy. Nothing more."

"His ... his feet."

"Are normal."

"The examiner ..."

"Was mistaken."

Oxendine's eyes betrayed him, but Reuben simply repeated. "Do you understand what I require of you? Or do you need to see my mark?"

"No, master!"

"Am I not an exciser?"

"Yes, master!"

"And are excisers not to be obeyed without question?"

"Yes, master!"

"Then obey, and you may live through this night. Now, come."

He hauled the innkeeper to his feet and pushed him toward the door, grabbing Asha's shoulder and keeping the boy behind him.

Fresh air washed over his face as the door opened, and Reuben followed Oxendine's large frame as they made their way along the side of the inn before pausing as they reached the back corner.

Oxendine turned around and gestured past the corner. "Seamus sleeps with the horses. He'll wake for sure."

"Where does he sleep?"

"In the far corner, by the way in."

Reuben nodded, following the direction of Oxendine's arm and so the innkeeper didn't see Reuben's fist as it connected with his temple; he simply collapsed like a dropped sack of potatoes.

Asha gasped and Reuben snapped around, thrusting out his arm in case the boy darted away. But he did no such thing, merely watching as the exciser reached into his pocket and pulled out a folded leather pouch. Opening it, he held it up to the light, running his finger along the rows of tiny pockets within until he found the one he was looking for.

He took the large blue pill and pushed it into Oxendine's mouth before holding his jaw together until he swallowed.

"Did you kill him?" Asha whispered.

"No. This will keep him asleep, and when he wakes he'll feel too relaxed to raise the town." At least, that was the plan. He hadn't exactly measured out the right dose.

"Good. He was planning to call out the guard."

The boy was almost certainly right, Reuben thought, but he wasn't going to silence a helpless man.

Oxendine's breathing settled into a regular rhythm and Reuben rolled him against the wall. A passer-by would see a drunk who was sleeping off his liquor, at least until the morning. By then, they had to be away.

Reuben tugged at Asha's scarf and pointed toward the barn then scampered, as low as his back would allow, across the darkness toward the single lantern that marked the edge of the stables.

As they paused beneath the amber light, their breath fogging before disappearing into the sky, Reuben scanned the back of the inn. No one and nothing moved though, in the distance, he heard a dog barking.

The stables stank as only too many horses in too tight a space can, but Reuben sucked in some of the fresher night air before grabbing the lantern and diving inside.

He stumbled over the prone form of the young hostler, thrusting out a hand to catch himself, but what he'd taken to be a wooden wall crumbled into rotten fragments as he grasped it, sending him sprawling with a cry.

For a moment, blackness engulfed him as he struggled to get onto all fours, pushing the writhing form of the stable boy away. Then, the light grew from behind him, and he knew that the lantern had spilled and lit the dry bedding.

Seamus jumped up, crying out in alarm, but instantly turned his attention to the fire.

"Come on!" Reuben snapped, grabbing Asha. "Where's my horse? Where's Lucifer? Where?"

Seamus ignored him, stamping on the burgeoning fire. Any moment now, the cry would go up.

There! Lucifer's unmistakable black face with its white streak poked out of a stall, illuminated by the growing flames.

"We've got to let them out!" Asha said. "All of them!"

"No time!"

"I won't come unless you do!"

Reuben grabbed the boy and threw him into the stall. He put the saddle on and then lifted the struggling child onto the horses' back.

He began leading Lucifer out, then tied the horse to the railing and turned back with a sigh.

As he did, he heard calls of alarm and, moments later, the clanging of a warning bell, but he darted inside and helped the hostler to release the horses before running back to Lucifer and clambering into the saddle.

Running figures emerged from within the tavern, and Reuben kicked at the horse's side, directing him away from the burning stable, shoving other animals away as they filled the space, their arcane silhouettes dancing on the surrounding buildings.

He put his arms around Asha, holding him tight as he urged Lucifer on. Maybe, just maybe, this would work to their advantage. If the guard on the south gate was distracted, maybe they'd get away.

And maybe the pursuit would be all the more furious because he'd burned down the stable. Once Oxendine was discovered and revived, there would be no doubt that Reuben was a renegade, and a posse would issue from the town the following dawn. Assuming the whole place didn't burn down overnight.

Figures began to flood out of the buildings, some glancing upward to confirm that the aurora had faded, others looking across to the chaos of horses, most trying to get as far from the flames as possible.

He looked back at the stables, guilt stabbing at him. It was only a building, but such things were much harder to replace than they had been, and it was rare for the new building to be as well put together as the old. Humanity was in a downward spiral, but Reuben had no time for introspection, so he encouraged Lucifer through the melee and toward the south gate.

The burning breeze followed him, his arm gripping the silent Asha to his chest, legs gently encouraging Lucifer to navigate his way. He was a wise beast, picking the most efficient route away from the inferno that was casting an orange, pulsing light on the buildings. Good grief, had he set fire to the entire town?

No time to worry. The gate was just ahead. An iron structure set within the timber palisade, Reuben cursed when he saw the man standing at his post, bringing his rifle to bear. It was a single shooter, but one round would be enough.

"Open the gate," Reuben called out as he brought the horse to a halt.

The rifle remained pointing at his chest. "Gates are shut after midnight. What's happening over there? What's alight?"

"Stables. I found my horse and reckoned we might as well head away since his accommodations have gone up in flames."

"You should be helping. Them's the orders."

Reuben regarded the man in the flickering light. Mid-twenties with the lean look that was so common these days, especially in the towns. His comrades had gone to fight the fire and left him to watch the gate. And he was nervous, though he kept the rifle steady. It was a good weapon, built before the fall. Probably small caliber. But a twenty-two will kill just as well from this range.

"My name is Exciser Bane," he said, raising his voice as he'd been taught at seminary. "Stand aside so I can release this deviant from his torment."

The guard froze, his eyes flicking to Asha. Reuben could sense he was wavering; he just needed a final push.

"Do you wish to see my proofs?" He began rolling up his sleeve.

The guard lowered his weapon and waved his hand as if shooing away a child as he backed away from the gate. "No, sir. I'm sorry, sir."

Reuben nodded imperiously as the gate swung open and he could glimpse the river bridge beyond. He thanked the guard and spurred Lucifer on.

And, as he passed through and the gate shut behind him, he heard voices calling.

They were coming.

7

BOSTON

Foundation Headquarters, New Boston

ZAK HUSTLED ALONG THE candle-lit corridor pursued by the echo of his footsteps and the rattling of the porcelain on the wooden tray he was carrying.

As he reached the door, he drew in a deep breath and glanced up at the brass plate. It wouldn't do to wake up the wrong shepherd.

But no, he was in the right place. He had the honor of serving Father Ruiz, so he knocked lightly on the door, as instructed, and then opened it gently so as not to wake the father suddenly.

A candle stub guttered at the bedside, and he could see Ruiz's large form inflating and deflating with a low rumble as he slept. Zak crept around the wide bed and set the tray down before moving silently around the other side and gently shaking the shoulders of the woman who lay there.

Her eyes flicked open, and, after a moment's disorientation, she recognized him and yawned, her limbs going taut as she stretched. Stepping back, he watched as she swung her naked legs over the side of the bed. She glanced over her shoulder at the bloated form beside her and, as her eyes met his, an understanding passed between them. They were both unwilling servants of the Council of Shepherds. But, unlike him, she couldn't be seen to be here when the building came to life. She would have to scuttle away to hide until called for again, like all the other young women in her position.

Zak couldn't help watching her as she walked toward the door, his eyes having adjusted to the low light, fixed to the gentle rhythm of her backside. She turned again at the door, gave him a smile and was gone.

Returning to the bedside, Zak rang the tiny brass bell and lifted the cover from the food. After a few moments, the man's nose twitched, and he drew in a deep, staccato breath.

"Isaac," he said, breathing out a miasma of stale liquor as he raised himself on his elbows. To Zak, he seemed like an impossibly old man, and he was certainly a survivor from the before times, but when he'd asked about the father's age in the servant's hall, he'd been immediately hushed up. As if it was sacrilegious to even contemplate such mundane questions about one of God's appointed shepherds.

This made no sense to Zak. If Father Ruiz was some kind of heavenly being, he did a very good job of pretending to enjoy the earthly pleasures.

Zak handed the tray over.

"No apples, again?" Ruiz said.

"Sorry, Father. Cook is sending Eduardo to the market this morning. He hopes the city has authorized more fruit to be taken from the store."

Ruiz shook his head, his jowls wobbling. "The city needs reminding that the honor it enjoys of being the seat of our Earthly presence must be earned and maintained. They must attend to our physical nourishment while we see to the spiritual health of the world. It's bad enough that we must eat wrinkled apples. I remember when they were fresh all year round."

Zak nodded, though he couldn't see how apples could be fresh in the springtime having been harvested in the late autumn. "Yes, Father. Cook added two extra rashers of bacon."

"Bacon is not an apple, is it?"

"No, Father." Zak had never eaten a whole rasher of bacon, so he kept a watchful eye for leftovers, wondering how hungry the man was this morning.

He busied himself pouring black coffee into a goblet and leaving it on the table before standing in his accustomed place at the head of the bed. It was as if the man felt some instinctive guilt at satisfying his hunger while preaching moderation to others, and so preferred not to be observed while eating.

The priest screwed up his face as he sipped at the hot drink. "The only thing I miss more than fresh apples is real coffee."

"Is there anything else, Father?"

Ruiz grunted, looking up with drips of egg yolk running down his chins, and gestured irritably to the side. "Go about your duties and return when you're done. I will dress myself."

Thank heavens for small mercies. Zak nodded and steeled himself for the worst part of his job. Mr. Hoffman, a teacher at the orphanage, had once told him that hundreds of years ago and far across the sea, it had been considered a privilege to empty the king's chamber pot. But this was now, and Ruiz was no king, though he acted like one, and Zak didn't consider it an honor to have to carry the heavy bowl to the communal bathroom, trying desperately to keep all the contents within the rim.

By the time he'd returned with the empty, cleaned pot, Ruiz had finished his breakfast and was buttoning up his black jacket over his protruding belly while looking out of the open window. The chatter of a campus coming to life drifted up from below as the air freshened the room.

Zak slid the chamber pot under the bed, then went about straightening the sheets. A maid would be in later, but he'd found that Ruiz preferred the room to look tidy before he left to go about his business.

"Father, is there anything else you need me for?"

Without turning around, Ruiz made a dismissive gesture. "I have no further need for you until three this afternoon."

"Yes, Father," Isaac said, turning and leaving as quickly as possible before heading down the three flights of stairs until he reached the under-servants' kitchen.

A compact figure bustled into view. "Ah, there you are, come on now, sit down, sit down."

Isaac smiled and found his usual place on the long rectangular table. "Thank you, Mr. Wong," he said, before nodding to the other servants sitting around the table. Only half of the seats were occupied, but that was usual — he'd only seen the table full on very special occasions and when other households visited.

The cook made a grumbling noise and fetched a large cauldron from the kitchen, placing it on the scarred, oak surface before ladling a generous portion into each of the pewter bowls.

"Right then, begin," Wong said, sitting down at the head of the table.

Zak had his spoon in the air when he heard a cough.

"We should say grace, Mr. Wong."

He groaned and looked over at the slight figure of Leon. A recent recruit from the orphanage, he'd clearly had his religious duties thoroughly beaten into him. Zak half expected the cook to dismiss the boy, but, after all, if word got around that they hadn't observed the formalities, there would be serious consequences.

"Very well, boy," Wong said, his long nose and large eyeballs giving him the appearance of an angry eagle. "You say the words."

Zak closed his eyes as Leon recited the familiar words and the aroma of hot porridge wafted up his nose, making him feel even more hungry.

When the boy finished, Zak was spooning oatmeal into his mouth before the last amens had faded away.

"Where's Jacob?" he said between mouthfuls, nodding over to the empty place opposite.

Wong shrugged his bony shoulders. "How should I know? Maybe he's displeased Father O'Brien again."

Zak winced in sympathy. O'Brien was known for his cruelty and even the other fathers avoided him if they could. Jacob had been late to breakfast before now, generally because his master had woken up in an ill temper and decided to take it out on the boy.

Much though he hated the fat pig he was forced to serve every day, Ruiz had never raised a hand to him, though he had no doubt the man was capable of extreme cruelty. But since he'd left the orphanage to come here a little less than a year before, Zak had seen Jacob arrive to replace Thomas who'd died of some sudden, mysterious illness. Or so it was claimed.

Zak had never been naive, but that lie had been exposed for what it was the first time Jacob had limped back to the under-servants' halls, his face wet and his back striped.

The boy hadn't appeared by the time Zak finished his porridge, and he could tell that Wong was worried, even behind his mask-like face. He could see it in the man's eyes.

"I'm going to check the dormitory," Zak said as he left the table. The others had all gone already, but none of them knew Jacob as he did. Either that, or they didn't care.

Wong nodded as he supervised one of the skivvies while she washed the bowls. "Good boy," he said. "Just stay out of trouble, right?"

"Yes, Mr. Wong."

He found Jacob in the dormitory, curled up on his narrow bed, knees under his chin. Blood soaked his shirt and his trousers lay on the floor where he'd dropped them. No one else was around, which was unusual, but then Zak was learning that his chances of a tolerable life were greater the more invisible he became. And being associated with a boy who'd angered his master so much that he'd been beaten this severely risked calling unwelcome attention to himself.

And yet Zak didn't hesitate. He could have been assigned to serve that monster. It had just been the luck of the draw that he'd ended up with the repulsive but relatively passive Father Ruiz.

"I'm sorry, Jacob," he said, sitting on the edge of the bed. He wanted to stroke the boy's hair but a childhood spent in a Foundation orphanage stood between him and his humanity. He wanted to ask Jacob how he felt and where it hurt, but the first question was crass and the second easy enough to answer. "I'll go get some water to clean you up."

Jacob hadn't moved at all by the time he returned with warm, salted water in a bowl that he put on the bare floorboards. Wong had promised to ask the housekeeper if she had a spare shirt for the boy because if he returned to his master with one that was torn, he'd get another beating. Such was the masochism that stood in for justice at the Foundation's headquarters.

"You must take your shirt off," Zak said. At first, he thought Jacob hadn't heard him, but then the boy lifted the tattered garment over his shoulders, crying as the cloth rubbed against his open wounds, and laid himself face down on the bed.

Red stripes crisscrossed his back and buttocks, and Zak gently bathed them in the salt water, apologizing each time Jacob winced and cried out. Still, no one came into the dormitory and Zak felt his rage building both at the mercilessness of the monster who'd done this and the fact that no one seemed to care at all about Jacob's suffering.

No one except him.

When he'd finished, he used the shredded cloth to dry the wounds, then he heard someone clearing their throat and turned to see Wong hovering just outside the door with a shirt that, while it was old and patched was, at least, whole.

He muttered his thanks, then helped Jacob put the shirt back on. "You rest here," he said. "I'll handle your chores for the rest of the day."

"Thank you," the boy said in a quivering, defeated voice. They were the first words he'd uttered since Zak found him.

"Oh, did I interrupt something?" a drawling voice said from the far door. "I'll come back, shall I? So, you two can finish ... whatever it is you're doing. I hope it's not something unbiblical, if you know what I mean?"

Zak shot a poisoned glance at the familiar, lanky, sneering figure who was watching them with an amused expression on his face. "Get lost, Karl."

"Or what? You gonna kiss me to death?" he said, before spitting on the floor. "Pah, you catamites make me sick. I've got half a mind to report you."

"No, you haven't," Zak said, picking up the bowl.

"Haven't what?"

"Got half a mind. But maybe I'll tell Mr. Wong that you were sneaking around the dormitories spying on people when you should have been scrubbing the chapel. That's your duty, isn't it?"

The older boy's face screwed up. "You wouldn't dare."

"Try me, you cockroach."

Karl made to move toward him, but Zak turned away and called out, "Mr. Wong, are you still there?"

And when he turned around, Karl had disappeared.

8

HIDING

LUCIFER ACCELERATED ALONG THE bridge that spanned the Mississippi, sand and dirt flying behind him to patter down on Reuben as he drove the horse on.

Dimly, he saw the mudflats pass by and then they were over the river itself. Even in the gloom, he could see the gulch the Mississippi had flowed through until only decades before, now shrunk to little more than a trickle. Elsewhere in the country, there was water in abundance — though mainly salt water — but here, as in so many parts of the North American continent, it was dry.

He glanced back to see faint lights bouncing up and down, riders following them along the bridge. They would have to be fast horses indeed to outpace Lucifer, though he was no longer the tireless young gelding that Reuben had purchased a decade and a half ago.

Finally, Lucifer reached the bridge's end and they emerged into an open landscape of decaying commercial buildings, rusting billboards and brown scrublands with anemic trees and thick beds of reeds. How soon before nature claimed this landscape and the only signs of human occupation would be contained within the walls of the town?

He looked to his right and saw a long, low building behind a rusting red sign that bore the letters *Romantic Adventures* which only remained because the sign was too high to easily reach. He could imagine what was in the building itself beneath its partially collapsed red corrugated roof, and it would offer plenty of places to hide. Except his pursuers would expect him to do that.

So, with one final look behind, he guided the horse into the reeds on the left, instantly regretting it as a swarm of biting insects descended on them.

Ignoring the evil creatures, he jumped down, helping Asha to the soft ground and leading Lucifer deeper into the brush.

"Where are we going?" the boy said, his first words since they'd fled from the burning stable.

"Away from here."

"Are those men chasing me?"

"They're hunting both of us for different reasons. If they find us, they'll hang us or shoot us, so we must get away."

"I'm cold."

"I'm sorry," Reuben said. "We can't stop."

The boy had lost his shoes in Oxendine's basement and Reuben could hear the slap, slap of his feet as Asha picked his way through the marshes, heading deeper into cover.

Finally, when he was satisfied they were out of sight of the highway, Reuben stopped them and found a place among the bushes and straggly trees from where they could look for pursuit.

He saw nothing, though he caught the glow of the fire on the horizon. He knew what the townsfolk must think of him. They'd sheltered him, and he'd betrayed their hospitality by setting the town alight.

They wouldn't waste time trying to work out his motivation, they would just string him from the nearest electrical pole or burn him alive. Him and the boy.

From here, he couldn't tell whether their pursuers had taken the bait and were searching the building on the other side of the highway. He didn't know how many of them there were. He didn't know for sure that they *were* chasing him, but it paid to be cautious. There were enough deadly things in this world that the unwary had been eliminated from the gene pool. Confidence and optimism were not survival qualities in this new world.

"I'm cold, mister."

Reuben put his arm around him, the boy's body trembling.

"We can't build a fire here," he said. "If you want to get warm, we have to move on."

He lifted the boy onto Lucifer's back and led them away from the highway, finding a dried up-river channel to follow. Here, they were able to move much more quickly, though he didn't trust the ground enough to mount, so he strode along as fast as he could, peering back every now and again. Truth was, he wouldn't know if they were being followed until it was too late, assuming that their hunters were at all competent.

"Dammit," he said, pointing ahead to where a bridge crossed above the creek. If they were being pursued, there'd be a lookout on the bridge, so they had no choice but to climb the other side of the gully and pick their way between the iron supports of what had been I-55 as it rose above the dying Mississippi delta.

In the slowly growing light of the pre-dawn, Reuben's eyes roamed the support struts rising like the legs of giants out of the dust. Around them, like splayed feet, were the camps of generations of wanderers, all long abandoned in one of the many purges by the authorities of Jackson or the Foundation itself.

The people of the towns regarded those who traveled with suspicion, preferring to huddle behind their walls and rely on their illusory security. Most travelers joined the merchant caravans that took regular routes across the country, replacing the system of railroads almost everywhere outside of those few places where some semblance of order had been restored beyond the towns and cities.

They crossed warily between the feet of the giants and over a railroad track which they followed, their backs to the glow of fire, until they reached a series of rusting hulks, some of them turned on their side.

Reuben looked up at the boy who was hunched over the saddle, shivering. He'd wanted to put many more miles between them and their hunters before they rested, but he wasn't sure the child would make it. He couldn't understand why — it wasn't *that* cold, and Asha hadn't looked particularly weak, aside from the malnourishment that was typical these days.

But his heart told him that if he didn't find shelter the boy wouldn't make it. He felt a stab of shame as his first thought was the relief of being rid of the burden, but he shook it off. Allowing him to die out here was no better than leaving him to the so-called justice of the next excisers to visit Jackson.

He threaded the horse between the cargo trucks until he found one that looked intact, its sliding door wide open. Jumping inside, he scanned the interior, taking the solar charger from his pocket and using its LED flashlight to check for anything hidden in the darkness. Two seconds later, he'd shut it off, then he lifted Asha inside.

The railcar had been used many times over the years and he was able to gather enough fragments of dry wood for a small fire. Taking his steel and flint, he bent over the wood, involuntarily wincing as the sparks flashed in the grimy interior, imagining unfriendly eyes looking this way. He'd chosen this truck carefully, believing it to be shielded in all directions, but light was a tricksy thing; like water it could find places to leak out unnoticed until it was too late.

On the third strike, the fire took hold, and he cupped his hands around the kindling; blowing gently until the flame took. The second fire he'd caused tonight, and he only hoped that this one would not also have catastrophic consequences.

Reuben tied Lucifer to the railcar's handle, looking past his flank to the half-lit train graveyard beyond, but seeing no sign of movement. If it wasn't for the fact that he knew he was being pursued and that there were riders from the town roaming the countryside, he'd be pretty confident he was well hidden.

He dropped the horse's nosebag into place and poured in two handfuls of grain before taking his pack and blanket roll from behind the saddle and climbing back into the car. He wrapped the blanket around the boy's shoulders and unpacked his cooking set. Stained and dented it was, nevertheless, one of his most treasured possessions. Tradespeople in the towns fashioned pots and pans from salvaged aluminum, but there was no mistaking the machined perfection of pans made before the fall.

He poured water into the saucepan and placed it among the flames before taking a strip of dried meat, cutting it into pieces and dropping it into the water alongside some dried pulses and herbs he'd foraged before arriving in Jackson. It would be a meagre meal, but it would be better than nothing and he could go hunting later, assuming they shook off any pursuit.

Asha leaned against the metal wall, feet warming on the fire and, for the first time, Reuben felt his body relax a little as the heat and aroma of cooking filled the space.

"What are you going to do with me?" the boy asked.

Reuben, who'd been staring into the crackling flames, waiting for the broth to boil, glanced across at Asha. He'd stopped shivering and now sat cross-legged watching his rescuer.

"Keep you from being killed," he said, sighing. How was he going to do that? He knew of only one place where Asha would be safe and that was over a thousand miles away. Perhaps there were other havens, but he'd never heard of one.

In one sense, the boy was lucky: at least his deformity was hidden. That had kept him alive so far, but no one escaped examination forever. And an examiner would see that his toes were fused together by webbing, giving them an inhuman appearance.

Perhaps a surgeon could cut them, but he'd never heard of one who had the skill to do that without leaving traces. He shook his head as his shame caught up with him again.

There was no atoning for what he'd done. He hadn't been forced, hadn't been under orders, he'd believed. And he hadn't noticed the polluting of his soul until it had almost overwhelmed him. What an evil fool he'd been.

In retrospect, he recognized the Foundation's brainwashing for what it was. He wasn't the first man to become convinced that some people weren't quite as human as others. That was the key that made it possible for him to do the things he'd done in the Foundation's name and, at the same time, convince himself he was a good man.

He wasn't. He was a dark soul searching in vain for any trace of redemption.

Reuben looked at the boy and forced a smile. "I'll keep you safe," he said. "I promise."

And he knew it was a lie as he breathed the words out.

9

MARSHES

REUBEN SAT IN THE open doorway stroking Lucifer's nose as the sun warmed the railway car. He put down the precious e-reader and deactivated it, the final page he'd been reading remaining frozen on the screen.

"Suffering has been stronger than all other teaching, and has taught me to understand what your heart used to be. I have been bent and broken, but - I hope - into a better shape."

Just as in the nineteenth century, suffering was at the heart of human experience. Reuben had benefited from an enlightened education as a child which, as with most children, had gone completely unappreciated — resented even — until looked back on through the lens of experience. Dickens was an insightful author, but he couldn't have imagined what had befallen civilization in the two hundred years since he'd written those words. Humanity had risen so far and fallen further so that the great man himself, were he to emerge from H.G. Wells's time travel machine, would think he'd gone back and not forward in time.

He shook his head, put the e-reader in his pack and looked out of the train car. Soon enough it'd be

too hot to bear, which explained why the metal boxes hadn't been permanently occupied, but he and
Asha would have to make a move soon enough and
put some miles behind them before finding shelter
for the night.

But the boy could sleep for a little longer. Somehow, his snoring had a soothing rhythm to it and
Reuben relaxed a little. Or perhaps it was the heat
or the silence. He felt no sense of danger nearby, the
only sounds being the occasional fluttering of birds
or the buzzing of insects.

It was pleasant, sitting here with his legs hanging
over the edge, running his hands around the horse's
chin. He could almost imagine that the world hadn't
ended thirty-five years ago, though the evidence
was all around him.

Yes, he could hear birds, but their rich variety had
been pared down to a few common species who
were filling up the ecological gaps left by those that
didn't make it. There were more kinds of crow than
of any other large bird: he hadn't seen a raptor of
any sort since the first aurora. The smaller birds had
done a little better, though they generally existed in
isolated areas, hemmed in by the harsh new environment.

Some species had survived by sheer, blind luck or
divine providence, a pair or two lingering in some
overhung outcrop. But most had been deliberately
taken underground by humans when the second
aurora hit and released when it passed. It would
have been the coup de grace, the killing blow, if not
for those few people with the foresight to save a tiny
fraction of the world's ecological diversity. Rumor
had it that a secret Ark still existed somewhere, but
he'd never heard tell of where.

Vermin had done the best since the fall, naturally. There was no shortage of rats or cockroaches, and the wary man watched his feet as he walked the Western deserts that now slithered with rattlesnakes. At least they ate the rats when they could get them.

And there were so many deviants. He'd seen rats swollen to the size of small dogs, others whose bite was poisonous and yet more who ran naked and blind through the surviving sewers and watercourses, their mutation passing on to their offspring, multiplying relentlessly. Exactly what their survival advantage was over normal rats, he didn't know. Perhaps the loss of sight was compensated for by more acute hearing or sense of smell. But they were a horror to behold.

But aside from vermin, there had been other winners, just as when the dinosaurs had been wiped out in a distant past that was becoming increasingly lost to the survivors as the flame of science burned low.

Bats, for example, had emerged from their hiding places in caves, tunnels and houses to multiply as insect species flourished without their normal predators. He'd seen cauldrons of bats millions strong following the grasshopper storms that had stripped the fields of crops, dooming the farmers to starvation. The bats had made little impact on the devastation, but they'd gotten fatter and bred until, as the grasshopper infestations passed, their numbers collapsed again. It was evolution at a previously unimaginable pace. And bats were no longer creatures of the night; now they could hunt by day with little fear. It seemed to Reuben that the flying things he saw were more often leathery than feathery.

Asha yawned, then said, "I'm hungry."

Good grief, the kid sure was demanding. But then, after all, he *was* a kid. It was written into the contract. In blood.

"You'll have to make do with some biscuits," Reuben said, groaning as he got to his feet and straightened his back. He found a pack and split it in two — they would both be on half rations for the foreseeable future.

The boy nibbled at it and pulled a face.

"I'll eat it if you don't," Reuben snapped. He'd picked up the squares of dried cookie when he'd passed through a small settlement fifty miles to the west of here. It had been his reward for killing the leader of a pack of unusually social coyotes. How the creature had become the alpha given its mutations, he had no idea. Its back legs were practically useless, but it had a cunning he'd never seen in a coyote before. Somehow, it had lured him into a killing zone where the animals descended on him from all sides. He was hard pressed to fight them off, but had returned to the settlement with ten hides.

He had received their thanks, silver and a pack full of way-biscuits but no invitation to stay a while, so he'd ridden on, heart seething at the relief on the faces of the people as he left. They'd needed someone like him to destroy the threat of the coyotes, but not to live among them, even for a short time.

So, he'd moved on, friendless, his eyes on the highway behind. Not that he honestly expected to see the excisers galloping along in hot pursuit. No, they'd ambush him in the middle of nowhere. They knew he was dangerous.

He sighed at the hopelessness of it all. If he escaped the town's posse, he'd still have his former brothers in the Foundation on his heels, dogging him with infinite patience. He'd never be able to truly relax until he'd faced them. Or disappeared completely.

But first things first. If he was going to be caught and executed, he'd rather it happened tomorrow than today.

The boy complicated things. Before he'd arrived at Jackson, he'd only had one set of pursuers and was only responsible for himself. Now he was also being hunted by a posse made up of angry men who would take no more interest in due process than the excisers to whom he was already condemned. And if he was caught, the boy was caught, and they'd hang from the same tree.

He twisted around to where Asha sat. Despite his protests, he'd eaten the entire biscuit and followed it with a swig from Reuben's canteen.

"Are we safe here?"

"No. We'll have to move on."

"Where are we going?"

"I don't know. For now, I'm going to get us lost in the bush and head for Flowood."

"Will we be safe there?"

"We're not going to be safe anywhere, do you understand?" he snapped. Then, he drew in a deep breath. "I'm sorry. You know, Asha, you've *never* been safe."

The boy looked down. "Because of my toes?"

"Yeah."

"I'm a freak, aren't I?"

Reuben shook his head. Ten years ago, he'd have said yes, but then he probably wouldn't have wasted time talking to the boy. "No, but some people think you are."

"Why? It's just skin."

"You won't understand, but it doesn't take much for people to see other folks as ... well, wrong. It's foolish, and we can't do anything about it."

So foolish, he'd believed it himself for most of his adult life. Prejudices didn't have to be rational to be deadly.

They walked through the scrubland side by side, leading Lucifer. Passing behind the remains of a car dealership, they picked their way along the banks of a dried-up lake that was now little more than an expanse of marshland.

The rotten corpses of trees lay where they'd fallen in the years after the second wave of radiation, the one that had almost dealt a killing blow to the planet. As with the wildlife, the largest organisms in the plant kingdom came off the worst. Reuben had seen the devastated remains of the great redwood forests of the West Coast with his own eyes. And he'd seen the effects of the Amazon's death in the rising sea levels that had drowned the coastal cities within two decades of the disaster. Though they'd been abandoned long before then, having become the abodes of ghosts and ruined people.

He led Lucifer past the great form of a beech tree whose upper branches spread around it like outstretched arms. Over the years, axes had nibbled at it, and they'd come across the remains of campfires as the tree was, piece by piece, transformed to ash.

It wasn't all death and decay, though. Nearby, a waist-high stand of saplings stood at a respectful distance like mourners at a wake, and waterfowl chattered in the pools among the tussocks.

"Tell me about your parents," Reuben said as they walked.

The boy's mood had lightened as the morning had passed, but he gasped at the unexpected question and his head dropped.

Reuben patted him on the shoulder. "I'm sorry. You don't have to talk about them, but maybe you'd find it therapeutic."

"What does that mean?"

"It might make you feel a little better."

"It helps you? To talk?"

Reuben grunted. "What would I want to talk about?"

"I don't know, but you are very angry."

"I'm frightened, boy. Not the same thing at all."

Asha glanced up at Reuben, the doubt obvious in his eyes.

As he thought of an answer, Lucifer stopped, lifted his head and snorted.

"What is it?" Rueben said, following the direction the horse was looking in. "Can you hear something?"

He handed the reins to Asha. "I'll go check ahead. If I don't come back, or you hear shooting, climb up and get away."

"I can't get up there!"

But Reuben ignored the boy and, pulling out his 1911, he ran toward where the horse had been looking, darting from one clump of bushes to the next and taking an oblique course.

He heard something moaning, something inhuman, then the snapping of wood and a rising groan.

Rueben hid behind a bramble bush, gently teasing the thorns aside so he could see through. He cursed under his breath.

A horse lay on its side, flank sinking into the soft, marshy mud, legs flailing as it tried to get to its feet. As it moved, he caught a glimpse of a man beneath, trying vainly to keep the horse's weight off his legs and hips.

A good man would have run out and immediately tried to help. The horse needed putting out of its misery as it had obviously broken a leg. And the rider would need to be tended by a medic, which meant taking him back to Jackson.

A wise man would skirt around the commotion, hoping it didn't attract any more attention, and then leave the rider to die.

A just man would walk calmly out and execute the rider along with his mount because he was obviously part of the posse sent to capture Reuben and the boy.

He automatically checked the Colt 1911, ejecting and reinserting the clip as his mind worked.

Then Asha walked into view.

10

GLASS

"HELP ME!" THE MAN called out as he saw Asha approach.

Reuben tore through the bramble bush, cursing as he caught his hand on a thorn, feeling warm blood running between his fingers.

"Get back!" he roared, gesturing to Asha who froze, then stepped away.

But the rider thrust a hand out and grabbed the boy's boot. Asha fell to the ground with a shriek, letting go of Lucifer's reins and, by the time Reuben had reached the spot, a flash of metal had appeared at his throat.

The rider was a middle-aged white man with a pock-marked face and a torn ribbon of skin where his ear should have been. His black and white beard was corrupted by the remains of his last meal and as he saw Reuben his mouth broke into a rotten-toothed smile.

"So, I guess I've found you. Ain't that just fine and dandy. And the kid, too."

Reuben looked down at the man. He was trying to disguise his agony, but it was clear in his eyes. Brave, though. Not to be underestimated.

"Let him go," Reuben said.

"Ha! I don't think so! Now, you're gonna fire a shot into the air so my boys will come find me and we can choose a tree to hang you from."

"Why would I do that?"

"Because if you don't, I'll slit his mutey throat in front of you."

"You're going to kill him anyway. I could shoot you now and ride away, so why don't we just try to be a little civilized? What's your name?" He was buying time to think of a way out of this that didn't involve Asha having his throat cut.

The rider scowled as the boy squirmed at Reuben's words, only stopping when the knife was pressed against his jugular.

"Glass. That's my name, but my boys call me Boss."

"It's your posse that's chasing me?"

Glass nodded. "I'm the sheriff. And I know who you are. You got the mark of the excisers, but I never heard of them breaking a mutey out of jail. I guess you're a renegade, but whatever your business with the Foundation, I'll be happy to let them know we brought you to justice. Don't you move, now!"

"You want my help, you let me put the horse out of its misery. You've still got the boy."

The man on the ground grunted, wincing as he held back the pain. Then he nodded. "Do it. Beast nearly killed me and he's worthless now. And fetch me my canteen when you're done."

Reuben slapped Lucifer on the flank and the horse moved reluctantly into the bushes, then he stepped toward the stricken animal.

Glass's voice followed him. "You sure are soft for an exciser, ain't you? Don't want your horse to see what you're gonna do? I'm beginning to think maybe that mark's fake."

Ignoring the sneering man, Reuben crossed to the other side and lifted the horse's head, whispering as its eye swiveled around, full of panic. Under normal circumstances, he'd have put a bullet in its brain, ending its agony instantly, but that would bring every hunter for miles around, and he needed time.

"What are you doing?" Glass asked, unable to see past the animal's rump. "Don't try nothing or the kid dies. You gonna shoot him?"

Reuben reached into his pocket for the rolled-up leather pouch and searched until he found what he was looking for. He'd gotten it in case something like this happened to Lucifer, but this beast's need was greater. He took the huge pill and found a smaller one that he slipped behind his shirt cuff before quickly shoving the larger tablet into the horse's mouth and waiting for the animal to swallow. "I'm sorry," he said. "It's not your fault you served a low-life like this. Now, it's time for your pain to end."

"What are you doing?" Glass spat. "Don't go wastin' no prayers on him. Just put a bullet in his dumb brain and get me out from under him."

But Reuben ignored him, remaining still and whispering words of comfort as he felt the horse slip into sleep, the familiar dark cloud gathering around him at his powerlessness. He waited a moment, then he ran his blade across its jugular and stepped back, overcome with sorrow. How much more death would he be responsible for? Even a mercy like this was one more chip in his soul.

The horse twitched and Glass cried out. "You cut his throat? Why didn't you shoot him like I said?"

"Because I'm not an idiot."

"Well, get me outta here or I'll do the same to the boy. And hand me my canteen. No funny business, you hear?"

Reuben grunted an acknowledgment and, as the man watched him, he unfastened the leather canteen, swapped it to his left hand, and then gave it to Glass after unscrewing the lid.

"Now, let the boy go and I'll help you."

Glass shook his head as he gulped down the water, wiping his beard and sighing with relief. "No, you'll fire a shot, and my men will come help me while they're preparing a rope."

"So, kill him, then. Get it over with and then I can deal with you. I won't take as long over it as I'd like, but you'll be begging me to finish you by the time I end it."

Asha squealed as the knife bit into his skin, a stream of blood running down his neck.

"Be still!" Reuben said, focusing on Asha's neck, panic rising. Had he miscalculated? Would this son of a bitch kill the boy just to spite him and damn the consequences? "Okay, okay. I'll do it!"

Glass eased his grip and looked lazily up at Reuben, eyes shining in triumph. "Well then, go ahead. But get on with it, my legs are goin' cold."

Reuben raised the pistol and slowly wrapped his finger around the trigger, pointing the weapon skyward.

And Glass fell back, unconscious.

Reuben swept forward and pulled Asha out of his grip.

Once he'd checked that Asha's wound was superficial, he retrieved Lucifer and tied him to the other side of the bramble bush from Glass's horse.

"Was that magic?"

"There's no such thing."

"Yes there is, I've seen it," Asha said, seeming to find comfort in distracting himself. The shock would come later, Reuben suspected.

"You poisoned him?" the boy asked.

"Not exactly. It's a product of science from before the lights. It sent him to sleep."

"Science *is* magic, isn't it?"

Reuben sighed. He'd owned an iPhone once. What would Asha have made of that, he wondered? And how useful would a smartphone be in this new world? Without an internet connection, not very.

"When will he wake up?"

Reuben shrugged, looking back at the slumped form of the man. "He won't get a chance."

He lifted Asha into the saddle and handed him the reins. "Take Lucifer along the trail a ways and I'll catch up."

"You're gonna kill him? While he's sleeping?"

Without answering, Reuben slapped the horse's backside and sent him ahead. "Don't go far, I'll be there presently."

He watched the boy for a moment, then took his hunting knife and kneeled beside Sheriff Glass's head. It would be the simplest thing in the world to finish him off here and now. Leaving Glass alive would set a hound on their trail that wouldn't let up. He knew the kind of man Glass was well enough, the kind who lived by his own corrupted morality, the kind who saw himself as the undisputed hero of his own story. Self-deluded, cruel and merciless.

But also helpless.

It would be foolish to leave him alive.

But it would also be wrong to kill him in cold blood.

Reuben sighed. The pill would keep him unconscious for several hours and, in all likelihood, nature would do his job for him as the cold, wet soil leached the life out of the sheriff. He'd be found by his men eventually, and it'd look as though he'd died pinned beneath his horse.

He got to his feet and used some wet grass to wipe the blood from the animal's neck. Yeah, they'd have to look real close to see that it had bled out rather than dying from the fall.

Finally, he checked Glass's saddlebag and his coat pockets, before finding the sheriff's weapon where it had fallen when the horse had come to grief. It was a Smith & Wesson, ancient but well looked after. He should have left it to be found by the posse, but it was too valuable, too useful.

He paused for a moment. He was being a coward, and he knew it. He should either finish the man off or help him. The exciser wouldn't hesitate. But he was no longer the exciser.

As he left the clearing, he looked back at the sleeping form.

"I hope to God you die, you son of a bitch."

11

CARDENAS

"I DON'T BELIEVE YOU!" Asha said, looking over his shoulder at Reuben as they emerged from the tree line. "People can't fly!"

"Not anymore, but they did before the fall. I flew several times."

They were looking over a flat landscape that, from this slight elevation, revealed itself to be a patchwork of crops, all different shades of spring green.

Running through the middle was a perfectly straight stretch where nothing grew. Dwellings were spaced evenly along the surface, each, it seemed, associated with one of the field divisions.

Reuben checked left and right, then guided Lucifer down the slight slope. It was getting late, and they would need to find somewhere to camp for the night. He'd considered staying in the forest, but he preferred to be able to see all around. His greatest fear was to be ambushed. And if Glass had been found — and he'd survived — the chase would be on. But they'd headed in an unlikely direction, and it was a big country. Maybe he could lose them and stay lost.

The boy must have lived a sheltered life indeed if he hadn't encountered any remnant of the airline industry. Thousands of planes had fallen out of the sky on the night of the first aurora, but tens of thousands had been left to rot at airfields around the country.

What had this place been called? Some weird name made up of other names stitched together. It began with Jackson, though it was some way from the shrunken town that had replaced the city. The only trace that remained was the line of (what to call them? Shacks?) that ran along what had been the runway.

He wondered again whether Glass had been found yet. Ever since he'd left the man, he'd regretted not finishing him off. Yet another reason to keep looking over his shoulder. And yet he knew, for the sake of his soul, that it had been the right thing to do.

As Lucifer carefully made his way toward the level of the fields, Reuben looked for somewhere to hide. The grain silo was obvious — it had presumably been a hangar before the fall, but was the only building from the old airport that remained, the largest intact corrugated metal roof for miles around. It would also be guarded by the local militia, so Reuben looked for somewhere as far away from it as possible.

No point heading directly for the farmhouses on the old runway, but he was hoping to find a small barn or shed somewhere in the fields. Grumbling to himself, he pulled his spectacles out of his inside pocket. He hadn't needed glasses when he was young, but eye doctors had gone the way of the chiropodists, osteopaths and pediatricians; a shrinking pool of old specialists without access to the equipment they'd built their careers around. As an exciser, he'd gotten the best possible treatment, but that wasn't saying much and, in the end, he'd found a pair in a secondhand glasses store that worked better than the ones he'd been given.

Even with them, he couldn't see as well as he once did. His reflexes were still fast, but every morning he awoke with a sore back and stiff limbs, feeling even older than his fifty-seven years.

For some reason, contemplating the steady disintegration of his body always brought Mariana to mind. He'd fallen in love with her shortly before his ten year duty as an exciser came to an end and he was about to apply for some land to build on and retire.

This promise of a second life as his own master was why he'd become an exciser in the first place — or that's what he told himself. He hadn't realized just what the soul-price of his silver hoard would turn out to be.

Mariana had been twenty years younger than him, born after the auroras had become more of a nuisance than the planet-destroying terror of the past. When the sirens went off, folk were now used to taking shelter until they sounded the all clear. At least in the towns. The country folk had to manage for themselves.

He was drifting. He had barely slept the night before and they needed to find somewhere safe. But even thinking of sleep made him feel exhausted.

Mariana. No, think of something else. Too depressing. She used to rub his back in the morning, making him feel a bit less of an old man. He was ninety percent certain she truly loved him, at least at the end. Either that or she was an actor worthy of an Oscar. Back when there was an Academy.

"Ow!"

He snapped awake, grabbing at the reins, his thighs tightening their grip on the saddle.

"Sorry. You fell asleep!" Asha said, twisting around to look up at him.

They'd veered off course and were heading toward the last of the farmhouses on the old runway. Candlelight flickered in windows made from old, double-glazed panels. And then Lucifer stopped.

A man's head appeared at Reuben's feet. He looked up, eyes narrowing, then glanced at the boy. Without saying a word, he nodded, then gestured for them to follow.

Reuben drew his weapon and looked around in the failing light. Seeing no one else, he elected to follow the man walking silently across the cereal field. It was as if he were still dreaming, and he wasn't afraid.

In a small copse at the field's edge, he saw a wooden shed of the type used to dry logs for burning.

The man stopped and pointed at the shed, then moved off into the trees. Reuben watched until the figure crouched a hundred feet away beside a mound as tall as himself and began feeding thin branches into it through an invisible gap.

"What the hell?"

"He's making charcoal," Asha said, twisting in the saddle.

"You think we can trust him?" Reuben asked, surprising himself. How could the kid possibly know?

"Yes."

The man at the mound paid them no more attention, but simply sat and watched and looked in the opposite direction, through a gap in the trees to the fields beyond.

He had no rational reason to believe they could trust the charcoal burner, but, on the other hand, he'd presented them with shelter and Reuben was exhausted. It was a case of either take the offer or sleep in the open.

Besides, he agreed with the boy. He didn't believe the man would betray them.

And, anyway, he was too exhausted to care.

He slept fitfully, his dreams ranging from phantasms of the happier life he'd yearned for to nightmares of being pursued, encircled, captured and tied to a pyre as flames enveloped him.

He woke up gasping in panic, arms flailing until he realized where he was. He lay in the darkness waiting for his heartbeat to slow, then rolled over to check on Asha, listening to his breathing. The boy was still fast asleep, but there was no prospect of Rueben doing the same, so he crept on all fours to look through the gap between the two rough wooden doors of the shed.

He could see the faint glow of the charcoal oven, but no sign of the man who'd been sitting beside it. After checking on Lucifer, he headed toward the light. He felt the grip of fear — his exhaustion had made him take a ridiculous risk by accepting the charcoal burner's help. Had he gone to summon the watch?

Reuben patted the knife at his waist and made his way outside. He glanced up beyond the treetops to see that there was no sign of the aurora, just the diffuse glow of the moon above the clouds. Keeping low, he made his way toward the burner's camp, his eyes fixed on the orange glow, wincing at every twig snap or rustle of leaves.

The heat coming off the smoldering wood warmed his face, and he looked around for any sign of the man he'd seen crouching beside the smoking mound. Reuben's eyes watered, and he rubbed them as he turned his back. As he opened them again, he caught a glimpse of a smaller glow at ground level.

"You lost, son? You won't be needing that."

Reuben had swept the knife from his belt as he strained to make out the figure sitting cross-legged on the dark forest floor.

The man got to his feet and ambled unconcernedly toward him, a long clay pipe hanging from his mouth.

He was unarmed, and Reuben quickly sheathed his knife, feeling foolish. "I thought you ..."

"What, gone and told the watch?" the man said before chuckling. "Now why would I do that? You in trouble? The boy, too?"

"You know the ordinances as well as I do. You're supposed to report strangers."

Again, the man chuckled. "Just as well I never saw no strangers then, ain't it? Name's Cardenas."

"I'm Reuben."

"And the boy?"

"He's Asha."

Cardenas nodded. "He's got the mark, ain't he?"

"What?"

"Mutey, deviant, take your pick. Oh, it's alright, don't fret. I didn't call the watch. The watch no friend of mine. You old enough to remember the before. You know it ain't right."

Reuben examined the man's face. Old, though hard to age precisely behind an unkempt gray beard, his skin was black as charcoal, his bright blue eyes spoke of vitality masking a deep sadness. Or perhaps that was Reuben's imagination.

"I remember. But we had our own problems back then, didn't we?"

"Sure, I reckon it's part of the human condition. You'd think we'd learn something after a monster like Adolf got his chance at power, but the Foundation, well, they're cut from the same cloth," he said, eyes glinting.

"If you've got a point, I suggest you make it."

The older man put his hands up, and Reuben noticed that his skin was white — the black on his face was from his work. "No point, son, don't you worry. Only, when I see a man riding a Foundation horse carrying a boy, looking for shelter but not heading for the farmhouses, then I get to thinking."

"Foundation horse?"

Cardenas's teeth shone as he smiled. "Sure, I used to be a blacksmith. I know a Foundation beast when I see one. Now, that either means you stole it so you could keep the boy from them or that you're a strange kind of Foundation man."

Reuben shook his head. Maybe the man was just astonishingly perceptive, or good at guessing, or playing games with him. Before he could respond, Cardenas laughed out loud, his voice disappearing into the trees.

"Ah, don't worry none. I knew about you before you turned up. Sheriff's men have been to the farms yonder, told everyone to look out for a renegade exciser on a black horse. Got a deviant kid with him. Glad you came my way, or you'd be looking up from the wrong end of a rope by now, I figure."

So, that was it. Good grief, they'd been lucky. "You're taking a big risk."

"Why should I care? I don't put much store on my pitiful life. You know what I did before?"

"You said you were a blacksmith."

"No, *before*. I ran an events company. Can you believe that? Weddings, conferences, that sort of thing. Loved that job. Fixed up cars in my spare time, so I guess I was lucky to have skills I could trade. But I lost everything in the first lightshow, you understand? Everything that mattered."

Reuben nodded. "Me too. It's how I fell into the Foundation."

"Thought about ending it a thousand times, but guess I've always believed the old lie."

"What's that?"

"That it's selfish. As long as I can do something to help other folk, then I should. Now I tend this coppice wood and they have charcoal for their winter fires and for the forge. But tell me, where are you headed?"

Reuben rubbed his eyes, the weight of the question settling on his shoulders. "North and east."

"What are you looking for, son?"

"A hiding place."

"And not just hiding from the sheriff, I reckon."

Reuben nodded grimly. "I was an exciser, once."

"I know that, son. And I know what you're looking for, though I don't know as you'll ever find it."

"What's that?"

"Redemption."

Shrugging, Reuben looked beyond the wood to the dark fields.

"But you gotta try. That's the point," the old man said. "The struggle. The Foundation knows you've turned against them?"

"Yeah, it sure does."

"So, you got them on your heels as well as the sheriff and his thugs."

"That's about the size of it," Reuben said, nodding.

"You'd travel quicker without the boy."

"I know, but I can't abandon him. Not until I find somewhere he can hide."

Cardenas's pipe bowl flared as he dragged on it thoughtfully. "Look, son, I don't know what you did when you was an exciser, though I can guess well enough, but I know a good soul when I meet one."

"I don't have a soul, Cardenas, I lost that obeying the Foundation."

The old man took the pipe from his mouth and slapped Reuben on the shoulder. "Then I guess you go find it. No soul is so shattered that it can't be rebuilt. That boy in there is one part, and that's a beginning. Look for the embers and blow on them, wrap your hands around them and bring back the fire. But then, I guess you knew that. Now, we gotta talk. I need some sleep, and I can't be here in the morning. And there's things you gotta know."

12

VENKATESHWARA

REUBEN AWOKE AS SUNLIGHT filtered into the shelter, then rolled over to see Asha sitting behind the doors, peering through the gap.

"He's gone."

"Yeah. We talked last night, his name's Cardenas," Reuben said, sitting up and brushing the junk off the back of his travelling coat. "Anyone around?"

"No. I haven't seen anything. I'm hungry."

Reuben opened his pack and took two of the precious biscuits out. "Here, eat one of these. We can't light a fire until we're out of this country, so it'll have to do."

The boy pulled a face as he nibbled on the biscuit. "Where are we going?"

"Cardenas said we should use the trees as cover as much as we can. If we can get to the old lake, we should be okay. He reckons the posse hasn't got the stomach to range much farther. Aside from the deputies, they're mostly farmers and there's work to be done in the fields."

"Did you really leave that man who fell off his horse alive?"

"I didn't kill him, but I sure hope he's dead."

Asha shook his head. "I don't think he is. And I don't think he'll stop looking for us. He was real mad. Madder than the people who took Mom and Dad away."

Reuben glanced down at the boy and felt the darkness rising within him. He'd been one of those who made the 'mad' people that way. Part of a system that encouraged the persecution of the 'other'. Their dehumanization. "I'm sorry, boy. We'll be safer once we leave these townlands behind, but we've got to get moving. I'll dig a hole; I suggest you use it before we leave."

A light rain fell out of a gray sky as they led Lucifer along the inside edge of the copse and gazed out at the next group of trees. A narrow strip of marshy grass separated the two and there was no way to avoid taking the risk, so they climbed onto the horse's back and scuttled across expecting the cry to go up at any moment.

But it didn't and, moments later, they'd found the shelter of the trees again and immediately lost themselves in this thicker band of forest. Reuben had no more than a vague idea of where they were, only that they needed to head north, skirting Flowood to the west, until they reached the old reservoir. He had a route map, but it was only useful for long distances, and, after all, it had been made before the aurora, and the years since had reshaped the country.

They pressed on, seeing nothing but trees, hearing nothing but the crunch of their boots on the leaf-litter as Reuben led Lucifer slowly forward.

Within an hour, they'd reached the other side of the wood and were looking out on a huge concrete ruin. A rectangular structure that may once have been a particularly well-appointed motel with balconies on two levels, it now looked as though a bomb had taken it out. Reuben couldn't see a single intact window and many of the balconies were surrounded by fire-blackened brickwork, with rust-stained rails, most of which had been torn off.

But dead though it looked, he couldn't be sure that no one lived here. Outside of the towns, many people scratched a living as scavengers and squatters, desperation driving them to thievery. It had become a way of life for some roaming groups, and so the towns had built their walls higher and the distrust for wanderers grew. America was now a barren country with tiny pockets of order in a sea of chaos. Except in those few places where some kind of government had been restored and the cities under the direct control of the Foundation. But the people there traded security for freedom of action and thought.

Rumor told of a handful of sanctuaries dotted around the country. Places where some measure of normality had been restored. He knew of one such place because he'd been there. The people of New Haven had taken him in when he'd been dragged into town draped over Lucifer's back, his plague ravaged body and mind fit for nothing.

They'd seen his mark, known him for what he was, and yet had healed and comforted him. He hadn't been privy to their debates — and they must surely have argued about it — but he suspected they'd only finally decided to help him when they found the graves of his wife and daughter where he'd said they'd be, and he'd satisfied them with his answers to their questions.

He sought some form of redemption, though knew he could never be forgiven.

God knows he wouldn't have been so charitable if he'd been making the choice. But they'd seen something in him, a purpose they could put him to, and they'd sent him east seeking one of their number who'd gone silent.

But now he had the boy.

They skirted around the ruined complex, staying within cover as much as they could, eyes scanning the shadows for any movement. In the end, they were forced to abandon the trees and follow a road that ran between the rectangular building on one side and a dried-up creek on the other.

Saplings burst through the cracked asphalt of the abandoned industrial park that would soon enough be reclaimed by the forest. In another hundred years, Reuben reckoned, the place would have disappeared entirely, apart from some ruined stonework and twisted metal.

As they walked, the buildings seemed to become even more decomposed, nothing more than columns of rotting iron pointing impotently at the heavens.

Reuben glanced across at Asha who tramped silently on beside the horse, barefoot. He wasn't dressed for walking in this country on a cold, wet spring morning. As they passed into what had been a residential area, Reuben spotted a ranch house that, while it didn't look inhabited, might have one dry room beneath its collapsed roof. They could stop here, light a fire and wait for the rain to pass. But his heart told him they were still in danger. Glass must have been found by now, dead or alive, and that would give the hunters a trail to follow.

No, the boy would have to remain cold and wet for now. Once the rain stopped, Reuben would unwrap a blanket from its leather cover and dry him.

An hour later, they'd crossed what remained of Route 25 and were making their way through what had been a suburban landscape of ranch houses. Asha was walking more quickly since they'd found a pair of sneakers among the trash of an abandoned camp. Rotten, threadbare and two sizes too big, they nevertheless comforted his sore feet.

As they warily moved along the crumbling roads, they caught only glimpses of the ruined homes behind screens of trees, their branches bursting with life. It was only because he'd lived somewhere like this back in the old world that Reuben could picture what it would have looked like then, when nature was kept in check by chainsaws and lawn mowers.

And then, finally, they were back in the countryside, having picked their way through the outskirts of what had once been Flowood, the town bearing that name now being a shrunken husk.

The landscape they found themselves in now was a virgin, pathless forest of young trees that was too thick in places to ride through, and it wrapped around them like a blanket, protecting them from any but the most determined trackers. And yet, he still had the feeling they were being followed. He yearned to climb up on Lucifer's back and gallop away, but the trees pressed too closely about them and became even thicker at riding height.

After walking for hours, feeling as though they were moving forward at snail's pace, Reuben yearned to have an asphalt road beneath his boots and, when he caught sight of something rectangular between the marching trees, he headed for it, quickening his pace.

"What is it?" Asha said, coming to life as he scurried along after the horse.

Reuben couldn't quite believe his eyes as they adjusted to the sudden bright sunlight. Rising ahead of them was an ornate tower with a look of Far East about it. The morning's clouds had vanished and where the sun hit the tower's side, shadows revealed columns, towers and minarets carved in the limestone and, at the very top, five gilded objects like daggers. And the air smelled of something he'd long forgotten.

It was like emerging into another place and time and Reuben found himself abandoning caution as he hurried toward the black iron railings that surrounded the entire compound.

"Wait!" Asha called out from behind. "We have to be careful!"

The boy's voice broke the spell and Reuben stopped, running his hand up the side of Lucifer's face as if seeking the reassurance of something he knew to be real.

And then he noticed. The grass had been freshly mown. And the railings were still intact without so much as a speck of rust visible. It was some kind of temple, and it was still in use.

He hurried around the fence until it turned a corner and ran beside a road that headed toward Flowood. He stood at the gate, looking inside at a paved courtyard with smaller towers that surrounded the large one he'd seen when he'd first emerged from the trees. From this side, he could see that it had three shuttered windows spaced evenly, one above the other. He yearned to look out from the top opening and get his bearings.

"What is it?" Asha said as he moved alongside Reuben and pressed his nose between the bars of the gate.

"Some kind of temple."

"It's not Foundation, is it?"

"No, this isn't their style at all. Who's that?"

Someone was moving toward them. Bald headed and brown skinned, he wore green and yellow silk robes that swirled around him as he hurried.

Reuben put one hand on his weapon, but kept it hidden as the man approached, panting.

"Namaste. I am Swami Jayashankar. If you come in peace, you are welcome."

"We seek only a moment's rest and to trade for food if you have it," Reuben said, noticing the swami's ample belly beneath his robes as he caught his breath.

Two other figures hurried from the direction of the building. Younger, fitter and more modestly dressed, they looked on Reuben and Asha with more reserve than the swami.

The older man said, "We welcome all visitors to the temple of Venkateshwara. Now, open these gates, Chatterjee and allow our friends to enter."

Reuben led Lucifer inside, and one of the two younger men stepped forward.

"Chatterjee will look after your beast while you are here. He will refresh the horse and bless him for your onward journey."

After a moment's hesitation, Reuben handed over the reins and watched as Lucifer was led away.

"Now, come inside and enjoy the welcome of the great Venkateshwara in his temple."

13

HANNAH

HANNAH WRAPPED A COAT around her shoulders and made herself as anonymous as possible while she headed for the streets of Mecklen. Having passed the buck to her, Snider had dismissed the court two days before, leaving Hannah to chew on the impossible problem.

And she'd had plenty of time to masticate. She lived in a former tobacco merchant's home that had, centuries before the radiation storms, been turned into a large, brick-built manor with colonial pretensions. These affectations had been torn down in the years following the second aurora. The iron railings stripped away to be added to the piles of scrap that were then remolded into the necessities of a post-medieval agrarian society. Everything from plowshares to rifle barrels.

By the time Hannah first encountered the house, it had been stripped back to the brickwork and, on warm summer evenings, the sweet scent of *Nicotiana* would waft through the place. As a Black woman herself, though from the other side of the Atlantic, she'd hesitated to have anything to do with the house at first. But, in the end, she'd decided that she could better respect and honor those whose unwilling labor had funded the building of this place by turning it to good use rather than allowing it to decay back into the clay.

Tobacco growing had been one of the first industries to re-establish itself, and several farms (she wouldn't use the word plantation even if others did) had sprung up around the town. So, as if humanity hadn't suffered enough from the radiation storms, there was always the reintroduction of a carcinogenic habit to give it a kick in the nuts.

But no one had objected to her moving in — it was a place of ghosts according to local legend — and she'd made one room on the ground floor habitable before gradually expanding into the rest of the house. That had been twenty years ago, and Argall's was now a repository for every piece of scientific equipment she could scavenge. There had to be other scientists — perhaps at the sites of the former universities — but she hadn't heard from more than a handful, all of whom had no better facilities than her own.

She'd devoted as much space as she could to her main passion of astrophysics, but there was little time to indulge in it, except in the monitoring of the skies for auroras and recording as much data as she could.

Data was the grain that science used to make the bread of understanding. That was possibly the most pompous thing she'd ever said, but it had struck a chord. Most of the current population had been born since the radiation storm, so she found herself having to explain and justify her work to people who had no grounding in the kind of education system that valued science. The children of Mecklen left school at fourteen to work in the fields and regarded

Hannah — if they knew of her at all — as some kind of sorceress or a witch. A witch with a secret monster hidden in her house.

Her mind flicked back to Roberto. She always felt nervous when she left the house, and that familiar surge of fear sent her pulse racing as she saw his damaged face in her thoughts. The kind of face only a mother could love.

No, he'd be fine. He knew the procedure and what the stakes were for both of them.

She tried to dismiss the worry as she walked along the trackway that led past her house, heading for the outskirts of town. Between the two lay a series of small fields laid out in a grid pattern. They'd been created by demolishing the old-world houses and sweeping away the rubble to be used or re-used elsewhere. As with everywhere in the former United States and across the globe, the population had shrunk to a tiny fraction of its original size, and people wanted to live close together for their protection. So, historic towns that had grown from a colonial nucleus before expanding over the past few centuries had now condensed again to their former size.

And they weren't growing now. With the enthusiastic support of Snider's predecessor as mayor, she'd organized an annual census and she now had almost two decades of data. And it showed that humanity's survival was poised on a knife-edge. If the birth-rate didn't rise, there was every chance that the species would be extinct within a hundred years.

As for why, she had parts of the puzzle, but not the whole. The auroras continued, though at a much lower level than in that first four-month period after the initial radiation storm. She'd hoped the last deadly wave would be the end of it. It had lasted two weeks, and most people hid underground like sewer rats, emerging to a world of browns and rotting greens, but some hope they'd survived the worst. And they had, but still the sky was dangerous, and the radiation caused a drop in both the fertility rate and the chances of carrying a healthy baby to term.

And life was tougher now. Tougher than it had been since the middle ages. Humanity was hanging on by its fingernails.

But she had other concerns today, so she put thoughts of the long-term future out of her mind and marched toward the center of Mecklen.

She reached the checkpoint at the town inner boundary, nothing more than an alleyway between two redbrick buildings. This street always reminded her of Maidenhead in southern England, where she'd grown up, and her throat thickened as she brushed away memories of long ago.

The checkpoint was a wooden barrier a few yards into the alley, with the two buildings rising up on either side. It could be easily barricaded if bandits attacked, and defended by only a few men who could pick off the enemy as they ran along the narrow gap.

She exchanged a greeting with the two guards. They nodded respectfully, but she knew they only did that because she was one of Snider's ministers. And, frankly, she didn't care. She was no more fit to help run the town than they were.

"What's the news about Gene Burrell?" one of the guards asked. "He gonna hang?"

Hannah felt her eyes narrow involuntarily. She searched her memory for the man's name. Yes, Jimmy Wilcox. Mid-twenties and born on a farm that had escaped the worst of the floods and the blight that followed. He was one of many that Sheriff Mendez had recruited since then to bolster his security forces.

"He hasn't been found guilty yet, Jimmy."

Wilcox's heavy brows rose in unison, possibly with surprise that she'd remembered his name. "Way I hear it, he confessed in the courthouse. Ain't that right?"

"He did, but it's not as simple as that."

"Seems to me, it's *exactly* as simple as that. Man stole from his neighbors. Least that should happen is he loses a hand, but I'd give him the drop if I was in charge."

The second guard, who'd been lurking on the other side of the checkpoint's wooden barrier sidled over, his glance darting up and down the street.

He was an older man — a survivor of the radiation storms. "I sure am glad you ain't in charge or we'd all be headin' straight for hail," he said in a thick Virginia accent. "Let the good doctor here go about her business. We got our job to do, and she's got hers and I, for one, ain't sad that I get to stand here on this fahn day while she decides what becomes of Gene. Always good to me and ma family, he was. Sure would be sad ..."

Hannah glanced from one to the other. Old and new, past and present. Maybe she could learn something from these two. Checking no one else was around, she turned to the younger man.

"Your family's farm escaped the flood, didn't it?"

Jimmy shuffled uncomfortably. "Well, yes. We only lost the east pasture."

"What would you have done if you'd lost everything, like Gene?"

"Well, I wouldn't have thieved from my neighbors, that's for sure."

"Even if that meant your family starved?"

Jimmy's expression betrayed his uncertainty, but he stuck his chest out and shook his head. "We got laws. If folks don't wanna abide by them, then they can go find somewhere else to live."

"Thank you," Hannah said. "What do you think, Chester?"

The older man shrugged. "I ain't paid to thank, ma'am. After all, I'm a deputy. But it sure seems a shame. Gene's a good man."

Hannah nodded her thanks to both men, then passed the barrier and walked inside the perimeter, her boots echoing along the alleyway until disappearing as she emerged into the bright sunshine of the inner town.

It always felt to her, as she emerged, that she'd made her way through Diagon Alley into a parallel universe. Outside, people toiled in the fields or hid in their houses, but inside it felt as though nothing had happened three and a half decades ago. Timber-faced houses lined the opposite street while, to her left, a small shale-built chapel sat on a grassy mound.

And then the spell vanished. If this was a parallel universe, it was one where the internal combustion engine hadn't been invented and people relied on horses, oxen and, as she had, shank's pony. There were some surviving trucks and cars, but they were precious and only used when absolutely necessary.

The problem wasn't so much the engines themselves, but the gas to fuel them. She'd heard that the Texans were working on getting their oil extraction and refining technology back on its feet, but hadn't gotten beyond reopening some of the most accessible sites with retrofitted Victorian-level technology. Refining it so it would power the surviving vehicles would be a huge challenge, though she reckoned they'd have more chance with diesel because of the relative simplicity of compression engines. It would be years, perhaps decades, before the oil industry was back on its feet. And then there was the problem of reinventing the automobile. And when that happened, she knew Texas would use its newly restored commercial power to its advantage. She wouldn't live to see cars driving along the streets of Mecklen as before the fall.

She'd reconciled herself to using her legs for as long as they lasted and the small chaise-cart and pony when she couldn't manage the long distance to town any longer. She missed many things about the old world, but the automobile, overall, wasn't one of them.

Hannah arrived at the courthouse, first climbing the granite steps with the stars and stripes fluttering proudly but impotently in the wind at the entrance to the building, then headed for the jail cells.

"I'd like to speak to Gene Burrell," she said as a guard emerged and looked through the bars.

14

THE TOWER

REUBEN FOLLOWED THE SWAMI up the wooden staircase as they climbed the tower. His boots lay at the temple door with his sword and twin revolvers, and he'd been given clean socks to walk the dark marble floors of the richly decorated first floor. But he wanted a chance to take a look at the lie of the land so, with apparent reluctance, Jayashankar had agreed to guide him up once they'd eaten and left offerings to the various deities. The food had been delicious, the dried apples quite the sweetest things Reuben could remember eating, and he found himself energized enough to climb the tower.

The priests had found a change of clothes and serviceable leather-soled shoes for Asha once he'd dried himself, and the boy was now admiring the temple with Chatterjee. Reuben had found himself regretting his decision to press on before dark.

Once they were alone in the tower, Reuben found it possible to ask the question that had been nagging him.

"I'm surprised to find you here, swami. I mean, we've passed nothing but abandoned buildings since we left Jackson."

"Oh, there are many dwellings in Flowood and even a market. We go there to trade." The old man turned as they reached a landing, catching his breath. "You are a Foundation man."

Reuben shrugged. "I was."

"You have their mark."

"I'm surprised you noticed."

"I make it my business to notice. And perhaps that is the answer to your question. It suits the local powers that we remain here as we are. We have been visited by the Foundation before but, so far, they seem content to tolerate our presence."

He began climbing, and Reuben shook his head. That didn't sound like the Foundation to him. Tolerance wasn't exactly a central tenet of their extreme brand of Christianity.

"I don't understand what you have to offer Flowood," he said, deciding to focus on one mystery at a time.

"Oh, that's quite simple. We operate substantial farms to the north and east of here. We are the breadbasket of Flowood, you might say."

As they climbed through a trap door to the next level, Reuben stopped again. "You run farms? How can there be enough of your people to cultivate the land?"

The priest turned, leaning on the banister. "Our people? Oh, you'd be surprised how many people will accept our authority if it means they have full bellies through the winter. You are familiar with Western history, I suppose?"

"Not particularly," Reuben said, scowling.

"Well, your ancestors came from Britain, did they not?"

"I suppose so."

"And the abbeys were the farming power of that land. I don't know that the peasants who tilled the fields really cared too much whether their crops went to the storehouse of a bishop or a secular lord as long as they got to keep enough to survive. It is much the same here and now."

He turned away again and hauled himself up the final steps until he reached the upper landing and threw the wooden shutters open.

"From here, you can see what we have achieved."

Reuben felt his insides turn over as he looked out on the flat landscape. In truth this temple was no skyscraper, but it was the highest building he'd looked out from in a long time, and he grabbed the shutter's frame to steady himself.

Trees marched away to the east but, beyond them, he could see the regular rectangles of cultivated fields, all various shades of green. North, the vast black mud of the former reservoir. Snaking through the center of it was all that remained of this part of the Mississippi river that had once fed it. But there was clearly enough water both in the river and soaked into the soil to make for a rich growing environment.

"I'll just fetch the key to the south window," the priest said, climbing back to the previous landing.

Reuben glanced down at his bald head as he descended. "Thanks."

Now that he was more comfortable with the height, he found he could lean forward a little and get a view along the road that ran past the temple. North, it merged into the forest as it headed for the dried-up lake.

South, it marched between the trees toward Flowood.

Ice flooded his stomach.

Riders — a dozen or so — were galloping toward the temple.

He looked down as, with a *thump*, the trapdoor to the next level shut.

"You son of a bitch," he growled, jumping onto the landing and stamping. "Let me out!"

There was no answer, and he grabbed at the metal ring of the trapdoor and heaved, but it didn't budge. It had been locked.

He could hear heavy footsteps hurrying down the stairs.

He cursed himself for his naivety. He'd been a member of an organization that used the natural human reaction to so-called holy places to make people feel a false sense of safety, and yet hadn't noticed when it was done to him.

They'd played him. Somehow, they'd managed to send a message to Flowood while they fed their guests, delaying Reuben long enough for the posse to arrive. He roared his frustration at the walls.

Then, calming himself, he looked out of the window again. How long did he have? Ten minutes, fifteen at the most, and the only way down was through the trapdoor or by simply jumping. And he'd take that over allowing himself to be captured. But what of the boy?

He looked straight down, satisfying himself that jumping would just be an efficient kind of suicide.

But if he could reach the shuttered window below...

And if the swami hadn't locked the trapdoor on that level...

His stomach turned as he leaned out through the opening, looking for any handholds.

The trunk of an elephant emerged from the cement a few feet down and, directly below it, a pair of parrots. From there he could jump onto the top of the lower window.

Assuming it would carry his weight.

One more glance at the riders on the road and he knew he had no choice. His heart thumping in his chest, he turned himself around, so he was straddling the sill, with one leg outside, then turned his back on the open air and lifted his other leg.

It was better that he didn't look too closely as he balanced over nothing, so he focused on the elephant's head and trunk, lowering himself, trying to find any kind of purchase with the tips of his shoeless toes as he went.

He swung, suspended between the window and the elephant for a moment before holding his breath and, grabbing at the animal's head with both hands as he dropped, his feet hung out over nothing but air.

He groaned at the scraping, pulling pain in his hands as he desperately searched for the pair of parrots. They were out of reach! He'd misjudged, and he was now suspended by his arms with no safe place to go.

Then the elephant's head quite suddenly gave way.

He yelled as he fell.

He yelled again when his feet hit the top of the parrot and the elephant dropped past him. Pain shot up his legs and his knees buckled, sending him falling to one side.

Reuben landed with a groan on the carved canopy above the second window.

This time he was ready for it to collapse under his weight, and he swung his legs in through the shutters and let go, hitting the floor inside and sliding against the wall.

He'd have given anything to curl up until the pain subsided a little, but the open trapdoor was just there. The treacherous priest hadn't closed it.

He pulled his weapon out of his jacket and half fell down the stairs until he arrived, in a mist of cement dust, at the bottom, an avenging demon.

As he emerged from the tower door and into the temple proper, the sound of shouting accompanied the slapping of his bare feet on the black granite floor.

Carven deities gazed down on him in disapproval as he ran, seeking the voices, seeking Asha and seeking revenge.

He found all three in the large chamber behind the wooden front door to the temple. Swami Jayashankar stood there, his hand clasped on Asha's arm as the boy struggled. The priest swung around at the sound of footsteps, then shrunk away, his back to the door as he saw Reuben rushing toward him.

"You bastard!" Reuben said, as the priest flattened himself and released Asha.

"I'm ... I'm sorry. Please don't hurt me!"

Reuben wanted answers, but he had no time. "Are you even a real swami?"

Any remaining color drained from Jayashankar's face, and he shook his head, his chins wobbling.

Reuben pulled at the door, flooding the interior with light as the priest fell away, disappearing into the shadows.

"We've got to find Lucifer," he said to Asha. "Hurry!"

He led the boy around the side of the main temple building in the direction he'd seen Chatterjee go, fearing that he might have ridden Lucifer to fetch the posse.

But no, there he was. Maybe they'd been reluctant to ride a Foundation horse. More likely they had some other means of alerting the town.

Next to Lucifer was a smaller, dapple-gray mare.

"Can you ride?"

"Yes."

"Good, this horse is yours now," he said, helping the boy into the mare's saddle and releasing both animals from the stable.

He mounted Lucifer and turned to face Asha. "You understand, if they catch us they will kill us?"

The boy nodded.

"So, we must risk everything," he said, as he steered Lucifer to the front gate. "They will see us, but there is no other way out. I'll do my best to lose them, so you must keep as close as possible."

He drew his Colt and kicked at Lucifer's flank, emerging onto the road and glancing right to see the riders no more than a few hundred feet away.

"Now! Ride!" he called to Asha as the cry went up.

15

THE SWAMPLANDS

LUCIFER'S HOOVES THUNDERED ALONG the road as he skill-fully avoided the cracks and tears in the ancient surface. How he yearned to let the horse have his head and leave the pursuing riders in the dust, but he could only go at the pace of Asha's new mount.

Another mistake. He should have left the mare and had Lucifer bear them both. But horses were currency in these latter days, and, besides, if they escaped the posse, they'd be able to travel farther and longer on two horses than one.

If they escaped.

Shots rang out and Reuben braced himself, but they whistled by — a combination of poor weapons and poor marksmanship — and then ceased. Ammunition was too expensive to waste when pursuing a target that couldn't possibly get away.

They passed the sad remains of an RV park on their left; decayed fiberglass and naked wheels, all trace of aluminum stripped away. Trees lined the other side of the narrow road as Reuben looked over his shoulder to see the riders gaining on them.

He had no choice, he had to do something, so he let go of the reins and sat up tall in the saddle, twist-ing to bring his weapon to bear. The horse's smooth gait made for a solid aiming platform, and he took out the two leading riders before they even knew it. The others broke, heading left and right to take cover, and Reuben glanced ahead before checking on Asha.

The boy's horse was struggling to match Lucifer's pace, reduced though it was. A good, honest pony that would cope with a long day's travel, but she wasn't suited to prolonged bursts of speed.

He fired two more rounds at the pursuers, who'd slowed, thinking they were out of range, clearly not recognizing the quality weapon he was using. One man fell from his saddle. One more who wouldn't return to his home tonight.

Reuben holstered his weapon, reached back and grabbed the mare's bridle then, quite suddenly, jerked on Lucifer's reins, sending him off into the trees on the right, disappearing from view before their pursuers could fire another shot.

Lucifer found his own path down into a drainage ditch that ran beside the road, then up the other side as Reuben saw and heard the hunters enter the woods. He fired another round blindly into the brush, hoping it would slow them down as they tried to locate him. Everything about the pursuit told him they were rank amateurs, but there were at least nine of them left and even amateurs can get lucky.

They emerged from the thin strip of woods onto a dirt track that ran alongside one of the fields he'd seen from the tower window.

The heads of people popped up as the two horses went past, and Reuben saw that many were old and all were thin, in stark contrast to the priests who, it seemed, were their masters.

Reuben knew the dried-up lake had to be ahead and that they daren't get caught with the shore cutting off their escape. So, again, he tugged on Lucifer's reins as they reached the corner of a field, heading, as far as he could tell, parallel to the reservoir. The hedge rose until he could barely see over it and, finally, he dismounted and led the horses along the field boundary, keeping low.

Ahead, the remains of a wooden house sat at a crossroads between four fields. Much patched up, it looked as though it was still in use, though whether for storing seed or housing people he didn't know.

He looked back to the end of the hedge to see a man leading a horse turn the corner, then dropping to sight along a rifle.

"Quick!" Reuben barked, dragging on the mare's reins until they were out of view.

People were moving with the slow purpose of mindless laborers, some carrying tools, others baskets of poor quality food, some men, many women and of all colors.

Some glanced toward Reuben as he emerged, but all averted their gaze as soon as he looked at them, so he pushed through, leading the horses and Asha around the back of the wooden building, then into a narrow band of trees that emerged into another field system.

He followed the edge of the wood toward what looked like a ruined settlement. There was no hope of outrunning their pursuers, so he would draw them in and, perhaps, pick them off.

It had once been a gated community, but the iron barriers had been stripped away long ago, and the homes ransacked and denuded.

He picked the most dilapidated of the houses, leading Asha and the horses into a back yard of blown concrete with a swimming pool that was now filled with junk and fetid water.

"You wait here," he said to Asha.

The room he'd led them into was just tall enough to accommodate Lucifer and the mare. They picked their way through the remains of the roof until they stood in the center of the house.

"I'll lead them away. If I'm not back by morning, then get on Lucifer and ride away."

"No! Don't leave me!"

Reuben bit down on his irritation. "We can either wait here for them to find us, corner us, and cut us to pieces, or you can hide with the horses, and I'll pick them off one by one. Now, hunker on down and say a prayer."

He looked up at the boy, then sighed and reached into Lucifer's saddle bag and pulled out a small revolver.

"Here," he said, giving the gun to the boy. "This belonged to someone very precious to me, so you must look after it carefully. Pull the hammer back, then squeeze the trigger."

Asha's eyes widened as he took the Ruger.

"Don't use it unless you're cornered," Reuben said. The boy would have next to no chance against trained gun users, but that was better than nothing. And Marianna had no use for it any longer. "Remember, wait for me here until morning."

He turned around, ran his hand down Lucifer's cheek, pressing the horse's head against his, and then strode away, not looking back.

He watched as the hunters rode warily in through the gap where the community gate had been. Most of them wouldn't be old enough to know what such a place was, but walls and fences were familiar enough, after all.

He'd taken position inside the roof apex of the tallest building he could find quickly, looking through the hole where an attic window had once been. His spare clip was on the dusty, sodden floor beside him, representing all the ammunition he possessed. He couldn't afford to waste any, and yet his Colt 1911 was hardly a high precision weapon. He'd have given anything for a Winchester Model 70 to pick off the attackers with. Those things were worth their weight in gold, vastly superior to the latter-day models. Five hundred years-worth of gunsmithing had been lost overnight when civilization collapsed, and it was only slowly being re-learned.

Then he saw them. Three figures running, backs bent into the compound, weapons swinging left and right as if they expected to be fired upon at any moment.

Well, Reuben wouldn't want to disappoint them.

The attic reverberated to the first shot, filling with acrid smoke as the nearest figure fell and the others scattered.

Good, they hadn't spotted where the shot had come from.

He lined up the next, but it took two shots to hit him, and more posse members snuck into the compound, dropping to the ground and crawling, commando-style, keeping close to the raised concrete troughs that had once lined the community gardens.

Eyes looked in his direction. Rifles followed. Time to go. He picked up his spare clip and slid back along the attic roof, feeling the rotting timbers yield beneath him. He had to lead them away, picking them off one by one, so he climbed down through the house and crept into the overgrown back yard.

Spotting movement, he fired off a shot and, with a cry, the figure fell. He ran like a phantom, his heart racing as he skirted the back of the next house, then along the side so he could look toward where the posse had entered the community.

Idiots. If they'd been experienced hunters, they'd have split into groups, but instead they'd been too afraid to move, which only made them all the more vulnerable.

"I see him!"

Dammit! He'd been too casual, too dismissive. He turned tail and ran as he saw figures rush toward him, expecting, at any moment, the crack of gunfire and the searing agony of hot metal.

He made it to the end of the gap between two houses, then turned and shot twice into the shadows. A cry rang out and he heard shouting and the pounding of many booted feet.

He ran again, then took cover behind a crumbling brick wall at the end of a back yard, and took down the first man to emerge into the daylight. How many, now? There had been a dozen, now perhaps there were half that number. So, only six to one, now.

He ducked down and watched as two figures approached. Where were the others? He'd worry about that later.

Waiting behind the brick wall, he tried to calm his breathing so he could listen. As an exciser, he'd trained long and hard to bring perpetrators to justice. Perpetrators being anyone who defied the Foundation. But he'd learned more during his decade of growing disillusionment. He was a hard man to kill. But all it would take was a single lucky shot.

Footsteps approached, and Reuben drew the knife from its sheath, sliding the Colt back into the holster.

The shadow rounded the brick wall and Reuben leaped, grabbing the hunter around the neck with one arm and plunging the knife into his back with the other.

The man's screams rent the air and he flailed as Reuben drew his Colt and felled the other man even as he tried to bring his weapon to bear. It was like shooting fish in a barrel.

So, what did that leave? Three or four if his guess had been right. And where were they?

Cold metal pressed into his spine.

"Reuben Bane, heretic, I arrest you in the name of the Foundation."

16

BURRELL

GENE BURRELL SAT DOWN opposite her at a table in the interview room. A beam of daylight illuminated the scratched plastic surface, and Hannah strained to focus on the ghostly figure of the former farmer until the guard put a gas lantern on the table and activated it.

"Take off his cuffs, please," she said.

The guard, who was now standing behind the prisoner said, "That's not standard procedure, minister."

"These aren't standard times, sergeant. Please un-cuff him and then leave us."

"I can't do that. He may attack you."

Hannah rolled her eyes. "Are you going to attack me, Gene?"

Burrell shook his head. "I couldn't fight my way out of a paper bag."

"I'll contact Minister Snider if I must," Hannah said, looking directly at the guard. "He tasked me to interview Mr. Burrell and report back as soon as possible. Are you going to delay me?"

She knew it wasn't fair. The poor devil was only doing his job, and she'd put him in a no-win situation, especially if Burrell did take her hostage. "Please," she said. "I'll take complete responsibility."

The guard grumbled as he released Burrell's hands, then looked back once more when he got to the door, as if she might change her mind. But she simply smiled and watched him go.

"You always were a brave one," Burrell said, rubbing at his wrists and rotating his shoulder.

"I'm not afraid of you, Gene."

The prisoner sighed. "Well, maybe, but that's not what I meant. You've been sent to give me the bad news."

"What?"

"Don't be coy, Hannah. I confessed to being a thief and Snider wants to see me dangling from the hanging tree. And what Mitch wants, he generally gets. Though I hadn't thought he was a killer. So, when's it fixed for?"

Hannah's chair creaked as she leaned back. "You haven't been convicted yet, Gene."

"No matter. But I figured you'd come to prepare me for the worst. Wouldn't want a scene in the courtroom, would we? Old Gene Burrell wailing like a woman—no offense—"

"None taken."

"I mean to say, Mitch wants the spotlight on him, not me. And he sure don't want any friends I may still have to make trouble."

"Is that what you're planning? To stir things up for the town?"

Burrell's face widened in obvious shock. "It's just as well you're a woman, and I like you, or you'd be on the floor by now for saying that. Mecklen's my home, my town. I was here before it had that name. Had a part in choosing it, I did."

"Sorry, Gene."

He sighed, seeming to collapse in on himself. "No, I'm sorry. I made this mess, I gotta face the consequences. You know what hurts the most?"

"What?"

"That Mitch is gonna win. I don't think he's quite smart enough to have fixed all this to happen — for me to be here, facing the noose — but he's sure making the most of it."

Hannah's mouth widened in a mirthless smile. "I don't think even the mayor could make the Potomac flood, Gene."

"No, but he could have helped us, couldn't he? We lost everything, Hannah. All we wanted was to be fed through one season and we'd have had seed in the ground and grain in the stores by the next year."

Hannah sighed and rubbed her eyes, the long walk finally catching up with her. "I know, Gene. He should have given you ration cards for all your workers, but ..."

"Yeah, well, he's always careful to keep within the regulations, isn't he? The letter of the law, not the spirit."

Hannah didn't know what to say. She liked Gene. He was a good man. But he'd stolen, and Snider was right that if he wasn't punished, it would set a dangerous precedent and the town's authority would evaporate overnight.

"What are we going to do, Gene?"

It wasn't exactly usual for a judge to ask the accused for advice, but nothing about the situation was usual. They'd had their share of criminal acts in Mecklen, but they'd generally been simple enough to deal with. Crimes of violence, if conclusively proven, resulted in similarly violent retribution. The town records listed punishments ranging from hand amputation for a thief who'd beaten his victim, through the castration of a rapist to the standard punishment for murderers — hanging.

Gene hadn't used violence, but his actions had caused genuine suffering for his victims and a lot of anger in the town. Most often, a thief's punishment involved putting right what he or she had done, whether that meant working in the fields without pay to replace stolen food, or having their possessions seized. But that often caused other problems — if the thief was working in the fields without pay, how did they afford to feed themselves or their families? It risked forcing them into the same act that had gotten them into trouble in the first place.

In the end, any punishment was as much about maintaining a sense of justice and consequences as it was about putting right the wrong. And so she'd been forced to witness amputations that only made it harder for the perpetrator to make an honest living and, in several cases over the years, a cycle that often ended at the hanging tree.

"What are you thinking?" Gene asked.

Hannah rubbed her eyes. "I can't see a way out of this. I won't see you hung, Gene. You're right, Mitch wants that, and some others in the community would agree with him. But I won't support that kind of brutality. He talks about how vital it is for justice to be seen to be done and I say amen to that. But killing you wouldn't be justice, and some people would start wondering how far the mayor would go, and whether they might be next.

"If you were a young man, it'd be simple enough. Five years in the fields or the brick factory would settle your debt to the town."

Gene nodded. "But I'm too old for that. It'd be a whole lot easier for you ministers if I just dropped down dead in my jail cell. Maybe that's Mitch's plan B. Just make me disappear."

"Maybe, though he hasn't said it out loud. A long jail sentence isn't on the cards, anyway. Keeping you in a cell just makes you more of a drain on the town."

Then her conversation with the two guards that morning sprang into her mind.

"We got laws. If folks don't wanna abide by them, then they can go find somewhere else to live."

"What's that?" Gene said, leaning forward.

"Sorry, I didn't realize I was thinking out loud. Jimmy Wilcox said it to me earlier."

"Jake Wilcox's boy?"

"Yeah, he's a deputy now."

"Well, his pa's got no love for me."

"But maybe he has a point."

"You mean to banish me?"

Hannah shifted uncomfortably in her chair. "I don't know, Gene, maybe." Suddenly, what felt like an answer no longer seemed so good.

"It's a death sentence, you know?"

"Surely, it's better than being hanged?"

"I'll take a quick end over a long, drawn-out death starving in the wilderness or murdered by bandits."

Hannah rubbed her temples, trying to stave off the incoming headache.

Gene Burrell sighed. "I'm sorry. This isn't your fault. I'll do it. I'll go."

"What? But you just said ..."

He shrugged. "I spoke out of fear, but I know that if I was to be hanged, it'd make it harder to keep the town together. And there's Mary, Josh and Waydon to think of, and all the others. With me gone, maybe they can make the farm work. It's still good land. Even better for all that new mud."

"Oh, Gene," Hannah said, as she took his hand and felt it shake beneath hers.

"You'll make sure my family is helped? If I do this?"

"I will."

"Mitch won't like it. He'll say you shouldn't be negotiating with a criminal."

"I'm not negotiating. You asked for something completely reasonable and I'm agreeing to it. Are you certain you want to do this?"

Burrell grunted. "Want? No. I'm too old to be relying on my own two feet. I'll be dead by winter. But I've given my life to this town, and if this'll help draw a line under what I did, then I'll do it. Just don't let Mitch take the farm, will you?"

"I'll do my best, Gene."

He looked her in the eyes and nodded. "That'll do. When do I go?"

It seemed as though just about the whole town had come out to see Gene Burrell leave. Sheriff Raul Mendez stood next to Mitch Snider as the mayor read out the charges Burrell had been convicted of.

People lined both sides of the highway. Most were quiet, keeping their thoughts to themselves, but a sizable minority jeered and booed as each crime was listed, gesturing angrily at the condemned man as he stood passively listening. But when the sentence was pronounced, other voices were raised in objection, including two of the witnesses she'd seen in the courtroom.

It stuck in her craw to have to admit it, but Snider had been right that this was a delicate matter. The majority of the crowd, it seemed to Hannah, wanted to see Gene punished, even though most would admit that he'd been stuck between a rock and a hard place. It was amazing how little empathy people could have when they hadn't had to face the same choice. On the other hand, if he'd been punished more severely, a sizable minority would have objected. And they were the older members of the community who also tended to be the more influential and powerful.

So, Hannah had found the least worst choice and Gene Burrell would be cast out.

His family weren't here. He'd been granted one night with them at his home, with armed guards at every door and window, and had said his goodbyes.

As he prepared to go, escorted by a squad of deputies, Hannah pulled him into a hug.

"I'm sorry," she whispered.

"Not your fault," he responded. "I shouldn't have done it. My punishment is fair. Look after my family, okay?"

She nodded, tears running down her cheeks, stepped back and watched as the old man walked along the highway to the jeers of his former community. He didn't look back.

17

KELLER

REUBEN BLINKED IN THE bright light as the hood disappeared and his captor walked into view.

"Keller."

"I'm glad you remember me. Your actions of late made me wonder whether you'd lost your mind."

Reuben strained at his bonds. He'd been dragged into one of the houses and tied to a wooden chair as the surviving posse members tended their comrades.

His captor was a tall man wearing the traditional black cloak of an exciser over dark travelling trousers; dust and grime showing where they met his boots. Reuben remembered him as an extremely fastidious man who wouldn't have appreciated messing up his appearance in pursuit of his quarry. But causing a little irritation to Keller was likely the least of his problems.

"Your mistake was leaving Sheriff Glass alive," Keller said, wiping sweat from his bronzed forehead. "He was quite helpful. And without the distraction of his posse, I doubt I'd have found you so quickly."

Reuben sighed inwardly. Every instinct as an exciser had told him he should have finished the sheriff off. Had he been merciful because he hadn't wanted to disappoint the boy? Did Asha matter *that* much?

"Don't concern yourself overly," Keller said, smiling. "I'd have caught up with you soon enough. You shouldn't have given yourself away when you entered Jackson. Which leads me to my business here. Where is the boy?"

"You don't expect me to tell you, surely?"

Keller faked a look of surprise. "It would be wise. You, of all people, should be familiar with the techniques I'll use to extract that information if you don't give it up."

"You always were a sadistic son of a bitch," Reuben said, looking the man in the eye. Keller was a good looking man, his skin untainted by the pock marks that framed Reuben's jawline. He was also ten years younger, having grown up in the first years of the new world.

It was pointless to defy the inquisitor, but defiance was all he had right now. He knew how this story ended, the only matter for discussion was how painful it would be.

"Save your petty insults. You should have stayed in the brotherhood, as I did, then this would never have happened. The governing council are very angry with you, Reuben. They gave you everything and you spat in their eye."

Keller turned at the sound of someone walking in. "Yes ...?"

"Merrill, master."

"So, what is it?"

Reuben recognized the man as a member of the posse. Merrill scratched at his ginger beard. "Johns needs medical treatment. I'm fixing to take him back to town."

"Have you found the boy?"

"No, sir. We found the horse, sure enough. A fine beast."

"You are to bring it here, then you may leave."

Reuben fought to control himself as the inquisitor turned to look down at him. If they'd found Lucifer, how was it that they hadn't also found Asha? The boy could have hidden himself, but not the mare. But then, maybe this Merrill was thinking of keeping the animal for himself. He didn't dare conceal the fact he'd found a Foundation horse, but a nondescript pony was a different matter.

The man departed, and Reuben could hear the groans of injured people getting to their feet and being helped onto horses.

"So, let us return to the matter at hand," Keller said, pulling up a second chair and sitting opposite Reuben. "Where is the boy?"

"Why does it matter? You were hunting me, not him."

"He is a deviant, an offense against God, and I will not turn a blind eye now that I know of his existence. I will find him, and then I will take his life one piece at a time in front of you and you shall experience how futile it is to defy the Foundation. And then I will take what's left of you back to New Boston and you'll face trial for your defiance."

He was enjoying himself now, and he got up, pacing the room in delight at the prospect of returning with his prey to great praise and reward. Then he stopped and swung around, a look of mock concern on his face. "Oh, but don't worry, it will not be a long trial. Your death, however, promises to be a protracted and public affair. All must know the price of defiance."

Reuben returned his stare. He wasn't going to give the monster the satisfaction of seeing his terror, though it was real enough. He remembered witnessing the fate of a so-called traitor to the Foundation, back when he was a new recruit. In his mind's eye he could still see the man's twisted face as the flames melted his legs.

Nodding as if he read Reuben's mind, Keller returned to his seat. "Tell me where the boy is, and I'll petition the council for mercy. You will still die, of course, but it will be quick. Relatively. Better to die by the sword than tied to a stake, having been robbed of your manhood."

Reuben ignored the man, keeping his eyes on him as the inquisitor looked at him down his long, bird-like nose. Keller's handsome features were counterbalanced by a lack of any detectable humanity and so he relied on threats and fear to fulfil his Foundation-appointed missions.

"No matter," he said, finally. "Xavier will find the boy."

Reuben's insides tightened. He hadn't realized there was another.

"Oh, didn't I mention Xavier? He is my apprentice. Unlike you, I am ensuring that my place in the order is taken by another when my time comes. And Xavier is very keen and very, very thorough indeed. So, since we are alone for now, why don't you explain yourself?"

"Why do you care?" Reuben spat. He no longer had any hope either for himself or the boy. All he had left was self-respect and that wouldn't last long once Keller unrolled his instruments of torture.

Keller got up and went to the door, looking out onto the now quiet communal courtyard before turning back to Reuben. "I am simply curious. You were the bright star of our cohort, destined to become a grand inquisitor and council member. In truth, I was jealous of you, though it is a sin, of course, and I would not have admitted it, even to myself. So, what happened?"

"It took a long time," Reuben said, sighing as he fidgeted to fight off the oncoming cramp in his bent legs. "But in the end, I had to bow to the growing certainty that what we were doing was wrong. It was inhumane, the work of Satan, not a loving God."

Keller winced at the Devil's name. "How can you say that? We learned the proofs in our first year of training! We are in the time of the Great Tribulation, awaiting the return of our Lord and the restoration of His kingdom. But he will not arise again until humanity is purged of impurity, like that boy you were protecting."

"Where is that in the Bible? The second part, about purity?"

Keller shook his head. "It is the council's job to interpret scripture for us. But if we allow genetic impurity to take a hold, then in a thousand years, when the Lord returns, he may find no true humans left to greet him. Surely you understand? We cannot permit the corruption of the genome. The enemy uses the auroras to cause mutations and we must hunt them down and eliminate them before they take hold. Do you wish for our species to become shrunken or cloven-hoofed?"

"I used to believe as you do, Keller. But 'eliminate' means 'killing', and that's generally of children. Over time, it rubs away at the soul."

Keller, who'd stood with his hands on his hips, began pacing around again, as if to swat away the blasphemy. "You speak of them as if they were human. I have no more pity for a mutant child than I do for a piglet or goat kid."

Leaning back in his chair, Reuben raised his eyes to the ceiling. Right here, it was more or less intact, though water stained and rotten. The staining spread toward a single area of perfect white in the far corner. That had been how he'd seen his mission — to defend the pure from the encroaching corruption.

And he'd pursued his task with vigor, even as his victims begged him for mercy, each pointing out how minor their child's blemish was. An extra toe or finger; eyes of a different color to each other; ears with points that could move like an animal's; webbed feet or hands. Small things, to be sure, but one rotten apple spoils the barrel, or so he'd been taught.

He hadn't noticed the darkness until it had almost entirely enveloped him. He'd still believed in the necessity of maintaining the gene pool, but no longer tried to fool himself into seeing himself as no more than a gamekeeper culling sick animals.

Then he'd met Celia. She was a young woman with dark brown skin who'd lived in the wild since being abandoned by her parents. She had two tiny horns, like those of a young goat, entirely invisible in her hair, but there, nonetheless. She'd come into the local village to buy food, trading the metals she scavenged for in the wilderness, and one of the merchants had taken a fancy to her, seeing that she had no protector.

He'd tricked her into a place where they were alone, and attacked her. She fought him off, but his fingers found the horns, ripping one from her head as she struggled.

She got away, and, though the merchant formed a posse, they never caught her. So, when Reuben arrived in the town, they showed him the tiny horn and it became his duty to hunt her down.

And hunt her down he did. He found her living in a cave on the side of a mountain. He should have killed her immediately — that had been his policy to keep doubt at bay — but he let her speak. She showed him the relics of the old world she'd recovered. Relics of *his* world. She questioned him closely and without fear about why people like her were killed out of hand. Did the fact she had tiny horns growing out of her skull mean she couldn't be useful? Were they an excuse for cruelty and isolation?

He should have stopped her, his rational mind sensing how dangerous this blasphemy was, but his heart knew that she spoke the truth.

When the time came to kill her, she submitted, laying her head on a table, her neck exposed.

And before he swung his sword, she forgave him.

That was the breaking point. The moment when two decades of indoctrination collapsed in the crucible of shame when faced with the gentle humanity of this woman.

He'd done the only thing that would keep his soul intact. He'd cut off the other horn with his knife and took it back to town as a token that he'd found her. No one questioned an exciser's word, or doubted that he'd killed her. Which meant that she had to leave, so there was no chance she'd be seen by the townspeople. He sent her west and, one day a few years later, he saw her again. And hers had been the voice that had spoken for him when he'd arrived in town

But he said none of this to Keller, who simply stood, rubbing his chin and watching Reuben closely. Then the exciser took in a deep breath as if waking from a long meditation session and turned to see another figure enter.

Xavier.

"What is it?"

"I'm sorry, master. I found the horse, but not the boy. He must have gotten away when the posse arrived."

Keller slammed his fist against the wall. "Fools! I told them to leave Bane to me! We'd have them both now if they'd obeyed. The world is falling, Xavier, when peasants no longer respect us as they did. And that is this man's fault."

He pointed directly at Reuben, his hand shaking. "You will tell me where the boy is or, so help me God, I will tear the truth from your screaming soul."

Xavier had crossed the room and was looking directly at their prisoner. "But master, our orders..."

"I know the orders, you idiot!" Keller roared, his face turning purple.

To Reuben's surprise, Xavier persisted. He spoke in a calming voice, placing himself in front of the exciser. "We were not ordered to waste time on a child. Let us go. We have a long journey ahead of us. The sooner we arrive, the sooner we can resume our mission. I'm sure the council will give you the honor of lighting the pyre, my lord."

"You are correct, of course, Xavier," Keller said, letting out a long sigh.

"Your indignation and desire for justice does you credit."

Keller nodded. "Thank you. Yes, we will begin the journey immediately. Please make the preparations."

"Yes, my lord."

Keller watched Xavier go, then turned to Reuben, not bothering to hide his anger. "You had your chance, Bane. Now, prepare yourself for an uncomfortable journey with your death at the end.

18

NEW HAVEN

ISABELLA SOTO WIPED THE dust from her face with one hand as she opened the door with the other, then stepped into the merciful shade. She felt as though even the shortest walk along Main Street left her as desiccated as a prune. And just as wrinkly.

She brushed the blown sand off her pants and kicked her boots off before walking along the hallway and into the small kitchen. Opening the refrigerator door, she retrieved the water jug before closing it up again and walking into the other room, pouring the cool liquid into a glass as she went.

"That you, Bel?"

A man's voice came from an armchair that had its back to the room, its occupant looking out over the back yard.

"Sure is. You want some water? Lemonade?"

"No thanks, I've got a drink."

"Nice and cool in here."

The main in the chair grunted. "Fishing for compliments, old friend?"

"How could you say that? I got all the reward I needed when you named the school after me." She flopped down on a wooden seat beside the armchair.

She'd known the occupant for thirty-five years. When she'd arrived here just before the second lightshow, he'd been the mayor, and he'd still been mayor until a couple of years before, though truth be told he hadn't been the same since his wife left two decades ago and headed east. Desmond Myers had given most of his life to this town and still wasn't at rest.

Former Specialist Isabella Soto knew about loss. She'd settled in New Haven with the love of her life, but the major had died a decade ago. So, she'd devoted herself to being useful to the people here. And the cool breeze of the air conditioning was her biggest contribution. Frankly, as the world had gotten hotter and hotter, it had become nothing short of lifesaving.

"Got any gut-rot?"

She smiled and took the pack off her shoulder, reached inside and pulled out an ancient liquor bottle, handing it to her friend. "Best hooch this side of the Rockies. I see you were prepared for my visit."

Soto watched as the old man filled two whisky glasses, both bearing the scars of three decades' use, and handed one to her.

"Cheers," he said. "What's the latest? Bob declared war on anyone yet?"

Soto chuckled to herself. Bob Riggs was now the mayor having waited in Desmond's shadow for fifteen long years. And the grasshopper plague had passed through in his first year in charge, leaving practically nothing growing in the ground. It had been Desmond's policy to store more surplus than anyone thought they needed that had saved New Haven from starvation. Perhaps Bob was now over-compensating.

"No, the folks from Ely went away without kicking up too much trouble. They know we've got the whip hand."

"Because of you. I bet Bob had the air conditioning on full throttle."

"Hah! Sure did. It was actually chilly inside. But the tech's simple enough. It's just a case of getting ahold of enough solar panels."

Desmond grunted and looked at her. Pretty much every conflict between New Haven and its neighbor to the south had the same thing at its core. In the months following the second aurora, Soto and the rest of the Army contingent had driven south to Ely and harvested every solar panel they could get their hands on so she could rig up a twenty-four volt power system for as much of New Haven as possible. At the time, Ely had been a city of ghosts, and the vast majority of panels were taken from empty buildings. But, as the town had been resettled, the "stolen" panels had become a little like the Elgin Marbles, a constant bone of contention.

Fortunately, New Haven was well protected by its curtain wall and almost entirely self-sufficient.

Bel settled down next to the old man and looked out on the back yard. "Looks good out there."

In truth, it looked like an entirely average garden with a lawned area and raised vegetable beds running down either side. Entirely average for the world before the aurora, but these were the only green plants she knew of outside the remaining farms on the town's outskirts. Irrigated by pivot drippers, they drew water out of the dwindling number of viable deep wells and it was only a matter of time before New Haven relied entirely on others for its food supply, making it vulnerable.

"I'm happy with the grass," Desmond said. "It tolerates gray water, even though it gets so little it ought to dry to a crisp. But we can't eat grass, and the vegetables aren't doing so well."

"Isn't wheat just a kind of grass? Can't you transfer the trait from one to the other?"

Myers shrugged. "If I had a lab and a trained scientist to run it, then maybe. But I've got no more technology that Gregor Mendel had when he worked with peas. Jesus, I miss her, Bel."

Bel Sotto had been expecting this. She hadn't had a single visit with Desmond without his former wife coming up, so she stopped herself rolling her eyes and simply touched him on the arm. "I know, Des."

"I'm sorry, I know I'm not the only one to lose someone. I just wish I knew what had happened to her. Do you think Bane will find her?"

Sotto grunted. "If it had been my choice, I'd have either left him to die or put a bullet in his brain."

"I know, but he'd suffered enough."

"Not as much as his victims. You put your faith in an exciser, Des. In what kind of a world could that turn out well?"

Desmond drained the last of his liquor. "You're probably right. But his pain and regret were real enough, I think."

"Well, it's true enough you're much better at reading people than me. I've always preferred machines."

"I'll try not to take offense," he chuckled. "But I can't help thinking she'd know what to do. We're close to a breakthrough, but a miss is as good as a mile. If we can't plant up the old farm fields with something that'll survive, then the desert will take over and the town will die."

Sotto took hold of his hand, feeling the rough, calloused fingers, and squeezed. "You know she won't come back, Des. Time you made peace with it. You can't bring your son back, and you can't change a decision you made all those years ago."

Desmond Myers nodded, wiping a tear away, then raised his empty glass toward the garden and the grave marker in the center of the lawn. "Hannah," he said.

19

XAVIER

HIS THROAT WAS HOARSE from screaming, but that was the least of Reuben's woes. Strapped into Lucifer's saddle, eyes screwed shut, he tried so hard to hide the pain, but the slightest jerk from the horse renewed the agony.

Keller had poured all of his sadistic, repressed madness into the delicate task of removing the mark of the excisers from Reuben's arm, taking a thin, excruciating slice of skin without cutting the artery beneath. His orders, after all, were to deliver the renegade alive and fit for questioning, but he'd pushed as far as he could, the perverse joy on his face obvious as he crooned in a mock-soothing voice, cutting away at Reuben's flesh.

Now, as they rode slowly through the watchful night, all Reuben had was pain, tears and a growing wrath that threatened to consume him.

He paid no attention to the direction they'd taken. He knew where they were headed, but wouldn't have cared in any case. All that concerned him was the searing agony in his arm. He had no doubt that Keller would have spent all night at his work if Xavier hadn't insisted they begin their journey. So, Keller had reluctantly bound the wound with a bandage soaked in liquor and, together, he and his apprentice had dragged the screaming Bane to Lucifer and man-handled him into the saddle.

They halted at some point in the night and Reuben allowed himself to be hauled off the horse and dumped unceremoniously on the damp grass.

As he lay there on his side, he watched without interest as Xavier made a fire, then assembled a tripod over it from which hung a small cauldron. He poured a liquid into it and crouched beside the fire, stirring it as Keller stalked around, full of restless energy.

"Here," Xavier said, pushing a small, round pill into Reuben's mouth. Keller had suddenly disappeared into the darkness and Reuben swallowed, not caring what drug he'd been given. "I do not approve of Exciser Keller's methods, but I have been assigned to him because he is effective."

Reuben looked up at the acolyte. He was a young man, barely in his twenties and with an oddly asymmetrical face.

"Oh, don't misunderstand me," he continued, responding to Reuben's obvious confusion, "he and I share the same aims, I would merely be more efficient about it. It makes no sense to me to waste time inflicting pain for its own sake when it only delays us. You will die in agony, but not at my hand. Unless you resist."

Reuben grunted, searching for any sign of humanity in Xavier's icy-blue eyes. But, in fact, he saw no emotion whatsoever. It was like looking into the face of death.

Xavier walked away and, by the time Keller had returned from his wanderings, the drug had sent Reuben into a fitful sleep.

He awoke to the sounds of movement, and, after a moment's blissful half-consciousness, the heat of pain erupted in his arm and he groaned.

"Be quiet!" Keller hissed.

Reuben raised the blood-stained bandage to his eyes, wishing there was some way to stop an agony he couldn't escape from. The exciser's mark had been burned into the underside of his wrist when he'd graduated from seminary, but that pain was nothing compared to the searing torment of having the skin peeled back and torn off.

The only hope he could find was in the decision he'd made not to allow them to take him to New Boston. He would not stand trial to be made an example of. He had no hope of escape, so he would make them kill him, and the sooner the better. But they were both clever psychopaths, so they wouldn't make it easy. They were probably expecting it.

His hands had been tied in front of him and his legs bound together as he slept, and Xavier wordlessly came over and tilted him into a sitting position.

"Here," the acolyte said, pushing another pill into Reuben's mouth, followed by the lip of his canteen.

"Food?" Reuben said.

Xavier smiled humorlessly. "We are only required to deliver you alive. I will medicate you because that will make it simpler to move quickly, but the master and I will share most of the food. You will get enough to keep you functioning, but no more."

Reuben watched Xavier get to his feet and move away.

Then, when neither of the Foundation men were watching, he spat out the pill.

Xavier and Keller ate something from their packs and then untied Reuben's legs and hauled him to his feet.

"Don't try anything," Keller said as Reuben faked the effects of the drug Xavier had given him. "There is no escape, but there is more pain in your future unless you obey."

Reuben treated him to an unfocused stare.

"How many did you give him?" Keller said.

"One, but it'll have more effect on an empty stomach."

"Perhaps we should feed him."

Reuben allowed himself to be half lifted into the saddle, showing no sign he was paying attention to the conversation.

"We have barely enough food as it is, master, unless we stop somewhere for supplies."

"No, we must avoid that if we can," Keller said, before looking up at Reuben in the saddle. "So, you'd better get used to being hungry, my friend. It won't be for too long, and then you'll never be hungry again."

Reuben ignored Keller, focusing instead on staying upright and suppressing the pain in his arm, fixing his attention on the trail ahead as the exciser and his apprentice mounted their own horses, Keller leading the way and Xavier following.

As they moved slowly forward, Reuben fought the temptation to break away, heading at right angles to his captors. Sure, they were both armed, both expert shots, but he suspected they'd kill him before allowing him to escape. That would, indeed, be the quickest way out of the nightmare of pain, but he had another need before that, the need for revenge. He would take one of them with him.

So, he sat tight, bore the pain and followed Keller's black horse as he led them along a rarely used track toward a young forest.

He drifted in and out of awareness as they rode, north and east toward New Boston and the end of his journey.

"Get him down," Keller said, and Reuben felt himself being pulled off Lucifer's back, waking only just in time to steady himself.

Xavier pushed him to the ground, and he gazed along the highway. It ran over an expanse of black and green, peaty soil that looked as though it would swallow any horses that strayed from the bridge.

"We must hurry," Xavier said, moving to stand beside Keller. "We can get across before dark."

"No, it's too risky. There is no cover until we reach the other side. Better we wait here tonight, then move in the morning."

Reuben remained slumped where he'd been left, apparently senseless, and listened. His captors had stopped several times over the hours and conferred without him being able to overhear.

"Do you seriously believe he has confederates?" Xavier said. "Who would help him?"

Keller grunted. "And yet we *are* being followed, are we not? We both agree?"

Reuben held himself perfectly still as he listened, biting back hope.

"They are simply seeing us off their land. They wouldn't oppose us."

"I'm not so sure," Keller said. "The sheriff is not the kind to allow a wrong to go unavenged."

"Perhaps, but he's surely not foolish enough to hinder an exciser about his holy duty."

"I'm not prepared to risk it. We will sleep here tonight and proceed all the quicker tomorrow."

So, Sheriff Glass's men were following them. Reuben knew he had no more hope of mercy from them than from the Foundation.

Xavier dragged on his arm and he pretended to be waking as he got to his feet. He allowed himself to be led toward what had once been some sort of motor vehicle dealership — probably something to do with boats given its location on the banks of the former reservoir.

Reuben glanced along the highway, back the way they'd come, half expecting to see riders, but there was nothing. The only way this situation could be worse, after all, was for Sheriff Glass to catch up with them.

Following Keller toward the building, Reuben could see that the windows had long gone, and the place was little more than a leaking iron roof on stilts, but one room in the far corner still looked largely intact. It had presumably been an office of some sort and had been inhabited many times over the years since the collapse. Though the door had been ripped off, the room was otherwise whole, aside from the remains of a fire in the center.

Xavier shoved him toward the room, sending Reuben staggering into Keller's back. Pain lanced up his arm.

And, finally, something snapped inside him.

He dropped his shoulder and shoved.

Keller let out a yell and spun around, his hand sweeping to the hilt of his sword, but Reuben swung his bound hands with all his remaining strength, heedless of the pain. He caught the exciser on the jaw, and Keller fell backward, sprawling on the filthy, rat-soiled floor.

Something jutted into Reuben's back. A pistol, probably, but he no longer cared. He spun around, catching Xavier across the face, and the apprentice cried out in surprise, stepping back and giving Reuben just enough time to break into a run.

He headed toward a rip in the outer wall, razer-sharp rusted metal framing what looked like a blast-hole, the boots of his captors thudding behind. As he emerged, he looked desperately for something to use as a weapon, but he saw nothing better than a long, decayed wooden bar, perhaps the remains of an oar.

Reuben picked it up just as Keller was on him, sword fizzing through the air in a blur. But Rueben, fueled by utter desperation and a hunger for revenge, brought the oar up as he ducked, catching Keller's wrist and the exciser roared in rage, the sword flying out of his hand.

Then, just as Reuben raised the oar to bring it down on his enemy, Xavier body-slammed him toward the lake's former shore, now just the division between dry land and mud-crust.

As he lay there, Keller rose like Lazarus, his face twisted in a rictus of rage, and for all of Xavier's protests, Reuben knew he was about to die.

20

ALONE

Yesterday

ASHA WATCHED THE MAN go with a mixture of relief and fear. Oddly, he'd felt safe around Reuben Bane, and yet never entirely comfortable.

He ran his hand along the mare's flank and patted her absent-mindedly then, for want of any better ideas, he wandered through to what had been the kitchen of the house before climbing the stairs to the mezzanine. Most of it had collapsed onto the ground below, and he felt a breeze against the back of his neck coming from a glassless window in the roof apex. At least it blew away the fetid stench of rotting wood.

Curious about what he might see if he looked out of that window, he went downstairs to find a wooden chair whose seat had collapsed. He brought it back to the landing and climbed up, feet on the frame's edge, straining on tippy toes.

Men, some on horseback, others already dismounted. Most of them looked like members of the posse, but two figures intrigued him. Both wore black and stood apart from the others. He knew they were excisers or, at least, the taller, older one was. And if he'd had little hope before, he had none now.

He trusted Reuben, but his friend probably didn't know about the two men in black hiding at the entrance to the collection of dwellings. Reuben had told him in no uncertain terms that he was to stay put and yet instinct told him that if he did that he would surely be caught and, soon enough, killed.

The last time he'd trusted other people it had ended in disaster. Jose and Esperanza had taken him in when he'd been found lost in the wilderness, but they'd been wrong to believe they could keep him safe in Jackson or that the risk was worth it for the promise of surgery on his toes. He was pretty sure it had been their contact in the city who'd betrayed them, and he'd been forced to watch as they were summarily executed before he was imprisoned in the basement to await the next exciser visit.

And now an exciser was risking his life to save Asha. It made little sense.

He watched the men outside prepare to enter the former community. What should he do? Could he rely on Reuben to kill them all? The former exciser was a formidable warrior, but there had to be a dozen of them, and he wouldn't even have known about his former brothers waiting in the shadows.

He'd been told to stay where he was, but Asha hadn't survived as long as he had by obeying the orders of others. No, he'd find somewhere safe to hide, and then come back if Reuben triumphed. And if he didn't? Well, that was a matter for tomorrow.

Asha ran down the stairs, suddenly full of energy now he'd made his decision, and stood beside the mare, wrapping his fingers around the small pistol Reuben had given him. He closed his eyes for a moment and tried to picture its previous owner, the one who'd meant so much to the exciser. An image of a woman with coffee colored skin and a sad expression emerged in his mind, but he had no time to dwell. Shots rang outside.

He whispered a farewell to Lucifer, grabbed the mare's reins and led her through the back of the former conservatory and into the back yard beyond.

A small copse of saplings had burst through the shattered cement providing cover as he led the reluctant horse toward the alley that ran along the property's border. Clogged with decaying wood and mud, he had to force his way toward the far corner of the settlement. His heart hammered inside his chest as he waited for the cry of discovery to go up and dreaded that he'd find no way out when he turned the corner.

More gunshots and the cries of pursuing voices. But not pursuing him. The shouts were behind, off in the far part of the former community. A high wire fence ran around this side, but it had long ago rusted into irrelevance, and he was able to pull it aside to make a big enough gap for the mare.

"Come on, horse," he said, yanking on the reins until they were both on the other side, standing beneath a cherry tree, blossom falling like fragrant snow as they forced their way through the tangle of branches.

They both came out the other side covered in pink. Asha wiped it from the animal's face and smiled, despite the peril. "That's what I'll call you. Blossom."

He tugged on her reins, and she followed him toward a decaying building. A rusting sign with half-vanished paint declared it to be a marina, though Asha had no idea what that might be. It had clearly been built on the shore of what had once been a lake, but was now merely an expanse of black mud cut through with green islets around which rivulets meandered, the higher regions dry and cracked.

He didn't want to take Blossom across that terrain, so he had to find somewhere to hide until the fight was over.

He headed for a single-story building that looked more or less intact, as gunfire echoed from somewhere behind them. Finally, he found an internal room that was dry and miraculously had an intact, though filthy, window through which he could watch the highway.

Of course, if he were to be discovered in here, there was nowhere to run to. But that couldn't be helped, so he brought the mare inside and found a position where he could sit and watch without being spotted from the road.

The gunfire finally ceased, but Asha didn't move from his hiding place. Most likely, the posse had gotten Reuben, and they were now searching for him. He was safe here, probably. And yet dread grew in his heart as he waited.

A couple of hours after the battle had ended, he saw several posse members mount up and ride back along the road the way they'd come. Six horses went back riderless and two had wounded men lashed to their saddles. But what about the two men wearing black? He looked and looked, but he didn't see them. He imagined shadowy figures flitting from house to house, trying to sniff him out.

But nothing happened.

Until the screaming started.

Asha sat with his knees tucked under his chin as Reuben's screams echoed in the night. He yearned to go to his aid, but he just couldn't do it. What would he find when he did? Those monsters ripping the flesh from Reuben's body? And what would they do to him if he revealed himself?

He gripped the small pistol. Could he kill them both? Could he save his friend? *Was* Reuben Bane his friend?

His mind snapped back to another night, four years ago. He could still hear the cries of his blood parents. He'd lived in the mountains with Mom and Pa not knowing the danger they were in until, one day, a group of men rode up the trail, spotting him as he fetched water from the stream.

He ran from them, but by the time he'd escaped, they'd seen the house. His mom had called for his pa, and had stood at the door with her shotgun.

Mom was so beautiful. Her eyes were blue and green, split neatly across the middle, but she'd had to pretend to be blind when regular folks called. Pa was much older. He'd taken her in as a child to save her from the excisers, travelling west to get away from the Foundation, and they'd fallen in love.

And Asha was the result. They never spoke of the webs between his toes, except to warn him that some people wouldn't like them, so he was to keep it a secret. They'd lived in the mountains for as long as he could remember until, that afternoon, the men had ridden in.

They killed Pa first, cutting him down with their swords after one had winged him. Then, they'd gone after Mom. She shot two of them, but that just seemed to make the survivors all the more angry.

Why had they attacked? Mom and Pa would have given them anything they demanded, but he didn't hear them ask for anything. They took Mom inside and he never saw her again. But he heard her screams, and there had been nothing he could do about it.

He looked down at the Ruger in his hands.

If he'd had it then, could he have killed them all?

Probably not. But he could have done *something* rather than cowering in fear.

And now? With Reuben screaming?

If he were to have any chance of killing both of the torturers, he'd have to choose when and how to attack them.

Until then, though it tore Asha apart to hear it, Reuben would have to scream.

Asha woke to the sounds of hooves on the dusty highway. He could barely see anything in the diffuse moonlight, but as he pressed his eyes to the glass, he made out the tall exciser on his black stallion, followed by Reuben, swaying drunkenly on Lucifer's back and the other exciser following.

He watched until they had faded into the darkness. There was no sense in following them immediately. Dawn wasn't far away, and the last thing he wanted to do was stumble on them in the dark.

So, he settled down to doze for a couple of hours, had something to eat from his saddlebag and gave Blossom some grain. He was just leading the horse onto the highway when he heard more hooves in the distance coming from the direction of the temple.

Panic and confusion paralyzed him for a moment before he came to his senses and slipped back into cover. Moments later, he saw a group of riders, some of them the same men he'd seen leaving the day before. But it was their leader that took all his attention. Sheriff Glass. His leg was encased in a rigid bandage and hung immobile from the saddle and his face was hard and grim and determined.

He saw another rider point along the highway and Glass nodded. After a few moments, they moved on.

Asha shrank away and slid down the filthy wall to sit on the damp, shattered floor. What was the point? Even if he could have ambushed the excisers, that would only make it easier for the posse to get Reuben. If he followed now, all he'd achieve would be sacrificing himself as well as the man who'd promised to protect him.

And yet he knew that he *would* follow, even if only to bear witness to Reuben's fate.

So, he waited for them to pass into the distance, and he followed.

21

BLOSSOM

ASHA SAT ON BLOSSOM'S back; eyes fixed on the high-way ahead. Twice, the horse had stumbled as the asphalt gave way, dropping into deep cracks that would, one day, replace the entire road surface. And twice he'd been forced to stop, lead her into the trees on either side, and wait for the posse to break camp.

The sheriff's men were in no hurry to catch up with the excisers, and this had puzzled Asha until he realized they must have known a place up ahead where they could either ambush their quarry or trap them.

The biggest puzzle, however, was how they could dare to defy an exciser. He'd never heard of such a thing. Granted, he knew little about the hunters of deviants, except to fear and avoid them at all costs. He knew they were relentless once on a trail and this was yet another mystery — surely they knew that Reuben was travelling with a deviant? So, why didn't they search for him? Why leave without finding him? His chief hope had been that he'd be able to shoot one of them if they came upon him, but he'd never had the chance.

Now, he was reduced to following a posse that, if they even suspected he were there, would ride back, trap him and hang him from the nearest tree. He was no longer just a deviant for the next visiting exciser to deal with, he was a fugitive who'd been involved in the wounding of their sheriff and subject to summary justice.

He lost sight of the posse at a long bend in the road and almost stumbled into their arms, but managed to guide Blossom off the track and into the densely wooded slope to one side, hiding a few tens of feet above the men. He heard the mumbling of voices and decided to risk staying where he was able to listen.

Peering between two boulders, he could see the large frame of Sheriff Glass sitting in a moth-eaten camping chair with his injured leg resting on a pile of blankets. Perhaps that was the reason they kept pausing.

"Don't you worry 'bout me, Silas," the sheriff's deep voice boomed out. "You fellas can chase them down and I'll come along to deal the final blow."

Another man, presumably Silas, tilted his head toward Glass, speaking so much more quietly that Asha strained to hear. "And you think we can sweet-talk them excisers into handing him over?"

"Like I told you, I don't plan on sweet-talking no one. They'll hand him over or ..."

A third figure leaned forward on the stony ground. "Or what, Sheriff? You ain't fixin' on ... on shootin' ... a ... a ..."

"Get a hold on yourself, Skeeter. You can say what they are out loud, they ain't demons."

"I've heard tales..."

Glass made a swatting movement with his hands. "You spend too much time with women, listenin' to their tall tales. Excisers are just men like you and me. And one of them ain't a full exciser anyway, he's just some kind of 'pprentice."

Asha could see only the top of Skeeter's hat as it shook doubtfully. He was obviously much younger than the others and his thin arms were visible resting on his knees.

"But if the Foundation ever finds out we've killed one of their priests, they'll set the city afire with everyone inside," Silas continued.

Sheriff Glass's large head turned toward the speaker. "Then we'd better be sure they're never found. You know how many bodies have been swallowed up in the mud flats? What's three more?

"Plan's simple enough, ain't it? Show ourselves when they're halfway over the bridge, then chase 'em down. They won't get clear across before we can pick them off with the Winchesters. But I sure hope that renegade is still breathing when we catch up with him. I've got words I wanna say before he gets turned upside down in the mud."

Glass returned to his meal, the debate at an end, and Asha climbed back down the slope. He knew what he had to do. Somewhere ahead was a bridge, and he had to get to it before they did, or he'd have no chance of doing anything to save Reuben.

He'd skirted the hill and brought Blossom down on the other side, meeting the road as it curved, then urged the beast along the edge of the wood, following the highway toward, presumably, the bridge.

For the next two hours, he gave half his attention to looking behind for any sign of the posse, and the other half checking for the excisers. And, finally, he saw the bridge. A wrecked building stood next to it with three horses tied up outside.

The highway straightened as it headed for the bridge, and the trees died away on both sides, so there would be no chance to sneak up or to conceal himself from pursuit. He could either hide in the woods, knowing that the posse would come by soon enough, or he could chance it, heading straight for where Reuben was being held.

He kicked Blossom into a trot, guiding her onto the more solid surface of the highway, then encouraging her into a canter and, finally, as much of a gallop as the pony could manage. The wind rushed through Asha's hair as elation, for the moment, overwhelmed his fear. He twisted in the saddle, but there was no sign of the posse. But he knew they were there, they were chasing and, at any moment now, the cry would go up.

And it did. But from ahead, not behind.

He could hear the sounds of a struggle taking place on the other side of the building beside the former lake.

There was no time to evaluate, no time to think. He drew the pistol from the waistband of his pants and ducked down on the saddle as Blossom turned the corner of the building. And there they were.

The tall exciser stood over two figures who struggled in the dirt beside the black mud of the dried-up lake.

As Asha brought Blossom to a halt, the standing man turned in his direction, shock and fear on his face, mouth wide.

Without hesitation, Asha brought the revolver up to eye level, wondering at how heavy it was in his hand, wrapped his finger around the trigger and pulled. It was much tougher than he'd expected, and the explosion threw his arm into the air, but, as his ears cleared again, he brought the gun down again. He'd missed!

The smaller man was almost on him!

He pulled the trigger again, and the small man disappeared in a cloud of smoke.

And Reuben was on his feet, throwing himself at the taller exciser as Asha urged Blossom forward, though there was no way he could shoot now without the risk of hitting his friend.

Asha could see fresh blood soaking Reuben's wrist and Bane roared with rage and pain as he grabbed at the sword arm of his attacker, half-rolling back and forth, the exciser spitting his rage up at him.

Looking down, Asha saw the crumpled body of the younger exciser, a knife laying beside him. He jumped down from Blossom and picked it up, running over to where the two men still fought.

The exciser was now on top, having wrenched his sword arm from Reuben's grip, and Asha could see the strength ebbing from his friend. The end was coming, and there was only one thing to do.

Asha plunged the knife into the exciser's back, then stepped back as the man roared in agony, the sword flying away to lodge, point down in the mud.

Reuben rolled over onto his knees as the exciser writhed.

"Give me the gun," he said to Asha who handed it to him wordlessly.

Reuben winced as he positioned himself above Keller, pinning him down as a red slick spread across the floor.

He held the revolver to the man's forehead. "You twisted son of a bitch, you deserve to die in agony or be left here to bleed out. But you know what? I'm not like you."

Asha watched as Keller's eyes went in and out of focus and then flicked toward him as he stood to one side of the two men.

"Does ... he know ... what you are? What ... you have ... done?"

Reuben pressed the snub-nosed weapon into the man's skull, hand shaking.

"We ... are the same ... Brother," Keller said, looking up at Reuben. Then his eyes found Asha again and he whispered one word. "Beware."

Reuben pulled the trigger and Keller went still.

"We have to go," Asha said, forcing the words out of a seized-up throat. He didn't know the meaning of what he'd just witnessed, but they couldn't remain here, that much was certain. "The posse is coming."

"Help me," Reuben said, then leaned on Asha as much as the boy could bear while he got to his feet. He held out his hands for Asha to cut his bonds, then he put his palm on his shoulder, looked him in the eye and said, "Thanks."

22

SKEETER

REUBEN LOOKED ALONG THE highway and cursed to the heavens. It was a cruel torture to believe he was rescued in one moment and condemned in the next.

There was no escape from the riders thundering along the road toward them. Even if they made it to the bridge, and even if their horses could outpace those of the posse, they'd be sitting ducks for a shotgun cartridge in the back, with no cover on either side.

But he wasn't about to give up and wait for death, not after all he'd been through.

"Come on," he said, climbing onto Lucifer's back. He'd taken his weapons back from Keller's mount. "Can you handle him?" He pointed up at the exciser's black horse, a twin of his own.

"I'll ride Blossom," Asha said in a voice that seemed to come from a long way away.

"No, she can't outrun them. We have no time, get up."

Asha shook his head. "She brought me here. I won't leave her."

"Suit yourself." Reuben glanced across the road to the bridge. And then he looked beyond and saw their one chance. A fool's hope. A black landscape of twisting creeks and little islands of grass.

"Head for the reservoir!" he called as he steered Lucifer onto the road, the shouts of pursuit going up as they emerged.

"But it's all mud! The sheriff said it swallows people up!"

"It's our only hope, Asha. Your choice. Take your chances with them or come with me."

Reuben glanced behind to see Asha following on the pony. Well, it was his choice and maybe where they were going, the smaller horse might be an advantage.

He kicked Lucifer forward, across the road and onto the grass the other side. Looking right, he saw that the posse was now no more than a couple of hundred feet behind them on the road, though the large figure of Sheriff Glass had been left behind, the white of his bandaged leg swaying comically from side to side.

Asha pulled alongside, his head bouncing up and down at Reuben's hip level as they made their way down the slope that marked the bank of the old, dried-up reservoir.

Without hesitating, and despite the obvious danger, Reuben urged Lucifer forward, but he was soon overtaken by the more sure-footed pony. "We need to get behind that island," he shouted as the clamor behind grew — he guessed the posse hadn't expected this and were waiting for their boss to arrive before deciding what to do.

Lucifer grunted nervously as his hooves sunk up to the fetlock. Reuben nudged him so he was now following the pony directly, walking in her footprints as she picked her way confidently through the mud, throwing up a rotten stench as she went. All the time, he expected to be punched from the saddle by a rifle round.

The voice of Sheriff Glass rose in anger, then was immediately smothered by the crack and rattle of rifle and revolver fire. Reuben bent down in the saddle. "Move!" he yelled, and the pony broke into a wet, sloppy trot with Lucifer following unsteadily.

Finally, Reuben jumped down into the mud and dragged the horse behind him as fragments of wet soil exploded all around.

"Stop!" Glass's voice roared. "Silas, you take Floyd. Get across the bridge and cut them off. Skeeter, you and Yates go after them."

"I ain't goin' in there, Sheriff!" A high-pitched voice called out in response.

"You'll go in there if I tell you to, you cowardly son of a bitch. Unless you want a bullet in the head right here and now!"

Reuben looked over to see the first pair riding onto the bridge and drawing level with them. One of them raised his rifle, but Reuben had just made it to the tussocky islet and any shot would be wasted. Ammunition was just too precious to waste on pot shots when they had their quarry trapped.

A pair of ducks exploded from the grass as Reuben brought Lucifer under cover and stroked his nose. "Well done, old fella." Then he looked over at Asha who was crouching beside him holding onto the pony's reins and shaking. "And, again, thanks. That pony of yours was a good call."

The child simply looked back out of unfocused eyes.

Reuben grunted as he watched the riders crossing the bridge. There was no way he and Asha could get across the mud before their hunters crossed, but he'd also be prepared to bet that the road didn't run along the bank of the reservoir on the other side.

If it did, they'd be sitting ducks.

"And I told you to stay put," he said. "Back at the settlement."

Asha shrugged. "Then you'd be dead, not them."

"Yeah."

He looked back the way they'd come as two figures walked along their trail, stepping in their boot prints even as they filled with water. One was an older man who came warily, his eyes scanning the tussock as if he expected them to open fire at any moment. The other was a young man so thin it didn't look as though his neck ought to be able to support his head. And he was terrified, his rifle shaking as he stumbled through the mire.

Reuben could wait for them to come into range and then open fire, but that would make it more likely the enemy would be waiting for them at the other side of the lake. He needed speed, but a bullet in the back would pretty effectively slow him down.

"They're behind that hill!"

Sheriff Glass had ridden onto the bridge and was pointing them out to the two men in the mud.

Instantly, the older man crouched so he was almost kneeling in the mud, and brought his rifle to eye level. The vegetation around Reuben exploded. So, they were in range after all.

He turned back to Asha. "Take the horses round the other side and head across. Keep this mound between you and the shooters. You got me? I'll catch you up."

Asha nodded, taking Lucifer's reins in one hand and Blossom's in the other, pulling them away.

A second shot thunked into the soil in front of Reuben as he brought his Colt up and a round fizzed past his right shoulder.

"Go get 'em!" Glass shouted, raising his fist. A pity he was too far out for Reuben to risk a shot.

The older man made a dart toward where Reuben lay, his boots slurping comically through the mud, his eyes wide. He fell to Bane's first shot and lay still.

Skeeter yelled and kneeled beside his comrade.

"No, Skeeter, you son of a bitch!" Glass roared. "Go get the traitor! Leave Yates where he is or so help me God, I'll put a bullet in you myself."

Skeeter looked across to the sheriff, then down at his friend and, finally, across at where Reuben lay hidden.

His face contorted in terror as he shook his head gently, gazing at the tussock before plodding reluctantly forward. He looked as though he expected to be blown off his feet at any moment.

Reuben's gut went sour at the prospect of killing this boy — shooting him like a one-man firing squad — but he couldn't leave him behind as they tried to make their way across the mud. Sure as eggs, Skeeter's fear of the sheriff would mean he'd take a shot at Reuben the instant he presented his back as a target.

But the man Reuben Bane had become wasn't the man he'd once been. If he were ever to redeem himself, even a little, he would have to face moments like this and pass the test. He'd have to immobilize this Skeeter without killing him. Somehow.

He glanced behind to see Asha leading Blossom and Lucifer away, shadowed by the bloated shape of the sheriff on the bridge. His heart sank. There was no escape. Even if they made their way across this stinking landscape, they'd find the enemy waiting on the other side.

He turned back to see the lanky figure approaching the mound where he lay hidden, rifle moving shakily back and forth, the squelching of his boots the only sound.

And then, with a squeal, he was gone, disappearing from view. Reuben crawled to the lip of the mound and peered between the reeds.

Skeeter had sunk into the mud up to his waist, his rifle flung away, and he was calling to the sheriff on the bridge as he tried to haul himself free.

Maybe Sheriff Glass couldn't hear Skeeter, or maybe he was a low-life scumbag who only cared about revenge, but he simply moved farther along the bridge. Yet again, Reuben cursed himself for not killing the man when he had the chance. Leaving people alive made for loose ends that came back to bite you in the ass.

So, he looked from the sheriff to the struggling young man in the mud, now sinking deeper, face white with terror where it wasn't spattered with brown. He should leave well enough alone and allow the lake to claim the boy rather than waste time rescuing him only to be encumbered with a prisoner he'd have to watch like a hawk. Rescuing the young man made no sense. After all, he wouldn't be in this desperate situation if he hadn't felt compelled to rescue Asha in the first place. Each time he chose to put others before himself, the universe rewarded him with a slap in the face.

But he couldn't — wouldn't — leave Skeeter to drown. And Asha was watching.

23

ROBERTO

"SOMEONE'S COMING."

Hannah looked up from her desk as Roberto stepped back from the window, the sunlight throwing the scales on his face into sharp relief. He looked like a thinner version of The Thing from the Fantastic Four except that this *thing* was a real human being, with just a few base pair sequences flipped. He was her monster in the attic, but she loved him every bit as much as the biological son she'd left buried in the arid soil of north Nevada.

"You know the drill," she said, as she reached the window and looked down to see a familiar figure striding along the track that led past her house. She had no doubt that Bobby was right, Mitch Snider was coming here. The only surprise was that he'd walked rather than ridden.

She reached the door just before he arrived, and had time to check for any signs that she shared the house before opening it.

"Hello, Doctor," the mayor said as he stood on the threshold. "Your garden looks lovely."

And it did. She'd spent a lot of time cultivating a front garden full of herbs, particularly medicinal varieties. As a scientist, she'd been skeptical — verging on the cynical — about the properties of plants, though she knew that aspirin had been derived from willow bark and that many natural substances had antiseptic qualities.

In this new world, however, she had no option other than to investigate the organic flora in the hope of confirming claimed properties and, perhaps, discovering others.

And it made for a beautiful garden. She even had a block of tobacco plants, though she didn't expect to find they had any health benefits.

"Come in, Mitch," she said, stepping back into the relative darkness as he passed inside. "Would you like some tea?"

"Thank you, that would be nice," he said, before his expression suddenly changed and he opened his mouth to speak.

Hannah got there first. "Don't worry, it's not my home brew. I bought this when Maisie got that case in from DC. Cost a fortune."

"I feel honored."

Filling the kettle from the faucet, Hannah gestured for Mitch to take a chair at the kitchen table. "You should. But you should give my brew another try, it'll put hairs on your chest."

The mayor's brow furrowed.

"It's just an expression. It's a strong brew. Pretty high in caffeine. Rumor has it, there *might* be a touch of nicotine in it. Oh, relax, Mitch. Don't take me so seriously."

The kettle began boiling and she poured the hot water into the tea pot. The first thing she'd done when she'd decided to make this place home was to find tea and tea making paraphernalia. Back then, it hadn't been too hard to buy tea bags or tea leaves left over from the apocalypse, but it had been years since she'd come across the real thing, except for the precious few boxes of PG Tips that Maisie had gotten in a few months ago.

She brought the tea pot over to the table and poured two cups, breathing in the warm aroma of what had been a bog-standard cuppa back in the day, but was now the drink of kings. She almost resented sharing it with Mitch who was, to all appearances, a Philistine in such matters.

"So, to what do I owe this rare honor?" she said as they waited for the drink to cool a little.

Snider looked over her shoulder at the bright kitchen window. "Actually, I'm not here. I'm merely one of the many apparitions this house has seen over the years."

"What are you talking about?" Hannah said, before adding, as the penny dropped, "Ah. Do you have a message from the other side?"

Snider's eyes darted around the room as if seeking out spies. "This isn't a joke, Hannah. Just remember, you didn't hear this from me."

"Okay," she said, resisting the urge to roll her eyes. "You were never here."

He seemed satisfied with that and sipped at his drink, before putting the cup back. "The Foundation are coming," he said in barely more than a whisper.

"What?" Hannah spat out her hot tea in what would have been a comical moment. But the Foundation was never a laughing matter.

"I got a message this morning from Frederick's Town. They'd had an overseer there for a week. He brought a squad of excisers. Hannah, there were burnings."

Hannah's jaw dropped open. "But ... but we're not a Foundation town. Virginia's not a Foundation state."

"Things are changing, Hannah. The new governor has ... connections with them."

"But burnings?"

The mayor went pale as he shook his head. "We know it happens in Foundation areas."

"How can the people in Frederick allow it?"

He shrugged. "Fear, I suppose. And the fact that it wasn't happening to them, as individuals. People become pretty selfish when they're scared that the finger might point in their direction. You know there are Foundation sympathizers here in Mecklen?"

Hannah shook her head. Had she been so blinkered that she hadn't noticed? A good scientist goes where the evidence leads; she doesn't ignore the inconvenient to preserve a pleasant lie.

"But look," Snider said. "I came to tell you because you may have to take action. You know, to conceal things you don't want the Foundation to find."

"Roberto isn't a thing!" Hannah snapped.

"Please, keep your voice down!"

"I'm sorry."

"I don't know who you're referring to, of course," Snider added in a conciliatory tone. "But I wanted you to have time to take appropriate action."

Hannah tried to force the tension out of her shoulders. This kind of stress wasn't good for her blood pressure. "I appreciate that, Mitch, I really do. Thank you."

He drained his cup and got to his feet as if, all of a sudden, he couldn't wait to get outside again.

As she opened the door for him, flooding the interior with bright sunlight, he turned and said in a low voice, "Be careful, Hannah. They're here to prove a point. I want no burnings in this town."

She watched him walk along the path. Thank God he'd warned her. Maybe she was a cynic, but she wondered why he'd taken the risk. Sure, they'd become civil enough over the years when not at loggerheads, but she didn't consider him to be a friend. He valued her as a useful asset to the town, and to him. He respected her intelligence and expertise. He didn't like her, as far as she could tell.

She shut the door and strode across the polished floorboards into what was now a parlor. Pushing a bookcase to one side, she slid the rug it was standing on aside to reveal a barely visible rectangular line that marked out a trapdoor. She knocked in her distinctive pattern *tap-tap tap-tap tap-tap-tap* and, almost immediately the door emerged from the floor, rising on invisible hinges. She didn't know what the tobacco merchant who'd built the place had hid in there that needed such cunning concealment, but she was grateful for it. Without this basement to hide in, she would have nowhere to keep her precious Roberto safe.

She fought back the shameful but familiar wave of revulsion as he emerged from the secret cellar. A thick bush of unruly brown hair was the only normal aspect of his appearance, his face a thing of nightmares. It was as if his skin was made of ice that had cracked to reveal a lake of blood beneath. Jagged lines crisscrossed his face, moving as the muscles beneath arranged themselves into what she'd come to recognize as a smile.

"All clear?" he said, emerging into the light.

"Clear."

"Who was it?"

"The mayor. He says the Foundation are coming into town tomorrow."

"Here?"

Hannah winced as the red lines stretched, blood moistening along the corners of his mouth. "Careful! Don't make it worse! Come on, let's see to you."

She headed toward the kitchen as Roberto followed, bare feet slapping on the floor. "Yes, they're coming here."

"But I didn't think ..."

"I know," she said, dabbing at his face with cooled kettle water. "We came here because Virginia isn't in their pocket. Or it wasn't."

He relaxed as she worked, dabbing oil on the rips in his skin. She'd never regretted taking him in, having found him as a small child when she was exploring the forests, making her count of species. She'd thought he'd been involved in some kind of accident, but it quickly became apparent he'd always been that way. He was four years old at that time, and all he knew was that his name was Roberto and he'd lost his parents though, in truth, they'd clearly abandoned him. He'd lived with them in some remote place that, from his descriptions, must have been deep in the new forests of ash, beech and fir that had sprung up to replace their ancestors. She had no idea what had happened to drive them to the sort of desperation that would be needed to abandon a child, but she couldn't leave him there and ride on.

So, she'd smuggled him back to her house and taught him how to hide in the basement. It was a poor life, trapped indoors except for the small area of the back garden that had been entirely enclosed. A poor life, but better than no life.

She'd spent the best part of the past fifteen years trying to work out what caused his skin to thicken and split as it did and to find a cure. If she could do that, there was at least some chance that, over time, his skin would heal enough that he could be allowed more freedom.

Mitchell Snider knew about him, though they'd never met. He used Bobby as leverage, and they both knew that one word from him would see both the young man and Hannah put to death.

And she was getting close to being able to treat his symptoms, if not the underlying cause, which was clearly genetic. He was no longer in constant pain, as he had been when she first found him, and the patches of skin between the tears were now largely a normal coffee color. But she hadn't found a way to heal the rips themselves so, though he looked much less repulsive than when she'd met him, he was still obviously a mutant.

The irony was that he was otherwise the healthiest person she'd ever met. He hadn't experienced a single day's illness. The viruses that swept through the town never touched him, even when she caught them, and he was left to nurse her. There was something about his immune system that simultaneously produced those disfiguring lines in his skin while also protecting him against everything else.

In another six months, she was confident she'd have a breakthrough, at least in terms of treatment. But there was a chance that a secret hid within Roberto that might just be the key to humanity's continued survival. All it would take would be a tiny improvement in survival rates overall to tip the balance in their favor. She'd find out, in time.

If the Foundation didn't find him first.

24

THE TOWER

ZAK'S NOSE WRINKLED AT the salt tang on the wind as he looked out from the tower of Foundation headquarters. He'd brought Jacob up here to escape from the cruelty and oppression of the former college below. The boy's physical injuries had begun to heal, but he'd only returned to Father O'Brien's service the day following the beating after the house apothecary had given him a calming draught of some herbal medicine.

That had been three days before. Zak had never been more terrified than when he'd knocked on O'Brien's door that first afternoon to attend to the monster in Jacob's place. But the priest had calmed by that time and hardly paid any attention to Zak as he'd gone about his duties, cleaning up the office and fetching him his afternoon drink and a pastry.

Zak suspected that the fact he was Father Ruiz's servant afforded at least some protection. He'd noticed that the shepherds tended to treat their personal servants more or less as if they were pets, and would take offence if another father treated them badly, even if they, themselves, felt no such restraint.

He came to the top of the tower whenever he wanted to escape everyone but, this time, he'd come to show Jacob the view. Somehow, it comforted him to see that there was a wider world beyond the confines of the Foundation headquarters.

"I've never been up here," Jacob said as he joined Zak beside the crenelated wall facing east. "It's amazing! Is that the old city?"

Zak looked out over a stretch of water that began just a few hundred feet away. The former Boston College was now a waterfront property, the Massachusetts Bay having swept inland. There, on the horizon, standing like the teeth of a sea monster that had died on its back, were a series of rectangular shapes.

"The old people called it downtown," he said.

"Does anyone still live there?"

"Not that I've ever heard."

Jacob shook his head. "How did the old people build such high towers? I mean they're bigger than this one, aren't they?"

"Yeah, much bigger. Mr. Hoffman told me some of them were seven hundred feet tall and had thirty stories! I don't reckon I believe him."

"Nah, no way."

"Well, the bottom floors are under water. There's nothing left inside them, as far as I know. No one's allowed to go inside anymore."

Zak led Jacob around to the north side. The water extended like a moat cutting off the grounds of the Foundation from the rest of New Boston.

"Where did the water come from?" Jacob asked.

"You know that. Or weren't you listening during lessons?"

"I want to hear it from you."

Zak smiled. "I was taught that it was caused by the sins of the old people. The rainbow lights shone in the sky as a sign that the promise God made after Noah's flood no longer held because man had fallen so low."

"Do you believe that?"

Fear flashed across Jacob's face as he realized what he'd said, and his eyes darted around in case someone might be hiding in the old stonework.

"It's okay," Zak said. "If you speak to old people — not the fathers, but people like Mr. Hoffman or Mr. Wong — they'll tell you differently, especially if they've been enjoying the cooking brandy."

Jacob laughed. "I found Mr. Wong fast asleep at the big table one night when I came down. The bottle was next to him."

"Well, he says that the rainbow lights were something to do with a star exploding hundreds of years ago."

"Stars don't explode. They were put there on the fourth day."

Zak smiled. "So the book says. But whatever it was, most of the trees in the world died, and that made the air warmer, and ice melted, and the sea rose. There used to be a huge jungle in the south and it just died."

"Why did that make the air warmer?"

Shrugging, Zak led Jacob around to the west side. "I dunno. I don't suppose it matters much, the water hasn't risen more in years, and they renamed this area New Boston. And the Foundation came and made it their home. Now, come on, I've got work to do. You can help, if you like."

Jacob made a grunting noise, obviously unwilling to refuse his friend.

"It's the girl's orphanage."

"Really? Sure, let's go!"

"You didn't tell me he'd be here," Jacob hissed, shrinking away as they almost ran into Father Ruiz as he stood in an outer corridor of the orphanage talking to a gray-haired woman.

The old man rotated like a forest moon. "Isaac, what are you doing here?"

"I have a duty, Father," he said.

The woman became aware of the two boys at the same time. "More likely you've come to spy on the girls. That's what boys do. Filthy."

"If you please, Sister," Zak said. "Mr. Wong sent me over. He said you asked for someone to clean the upper windows."

The woman's eyebrows almost met in the middle as she sought a way to acknowledge this without apologizing. Zak had noticed that children, and servants in general, were expected to say they were sorry even when it wasn't their fault. Foundationers, however, rarely apologized when it *was* their fault, and never to a child.

"You know this boy, Father?" she asked unnecessarily.

"He is my personal servant, regrettably."

Zak scowled inwardly. Regrettably? Sure, but not for Ruiz.

"And the other?"

"He serves Father O'Brien," Ruiz said.

The rictus of annoyance on the sister's face was cut off at the mention of O'Brien's name. Her eyes flicked over to where Jacob cowered against the wall.

After a few seconds, she nodded. "Then go about your work. Find Sister Noel and ask her to show you the tool room."

Without needing to be told twice, Zak raced off along the corridor. It was only when he'd rounded the first corner that he realized he didn't know who Sister Noel was and where she might be found.

Eventually they found her in the refectory. She was on her knees polishing the floor. Zak was so surprised to find a sister carrying out such menial work that, at first, he thought he might have been misdirected, and he was even more certain when she sat up on her haunches and revealed herself to be young — no more than a few years older than he was. And she was pretty.

"What do you want, boy?" she snapped.

"I'm ... I'm looking for Sister Noel."

The young woman sighed. "What menial task did Sister Greer send you to inform me of?"

"She said we were to ask you where the window cleaning tools are. Mr. Wong sent us over."

"To do what?"

He couldn't think of any cooler way to put it. "To clean your windows, Sister. Like I said, Mr. Wong sent us."

"Did he now?" she said, tilting her head. "And who is your silent friend?"

Zak gestured as casually as he could. "This is Jacob."

"Hello, Jacob," she said, smiling at him.

Jacob went bright red and murmured a response.

"Well, if Mr. Wong wants you to clean the windows, he must be talking about the ones in the worship room, mustn't he?"

"Yes, Sister." Zak had no idea if that was true, but wasn't about to admit it.

"In which case, you'd better run along and get the inside work done before the one p.m. service. But don't forget you'll have to climb on the roof to clean the outside. You'll have to be very careful not to disturb the service, so I suggest you work as quickly as possible, then hide in the roof until everyone's gone."

Zak nodded, though he wasn't sure he understood exactly.

"Everyone, you understand?"

"Yes, Sister."

"You know our principle; the work must be done for its own sake and not because we wish for reward. Yes?"

Again, Zak nodded. He felt as though there was something about all of this that he hadn't grasped, but he kept it to himself.

"Even a sister like me must do it. That's why you find me on my hands and knees scrubbing the floor while Sister Greer enjoys tea with Father Ruiz."

This time, he recognized the emotion behind the words, but kept his mouth shut.

"Yes, Sister, thank you."

"Well, hurry along, then. Or you won't be finished in time."

As Zak moved away, he looked over his shoulder to see the young Sister looking back at him.

25

MARSHES

As NIGHT FELL, REUBEN, Asha and Skeeter made camp on a small island in the wilderness. Asha and Blossom had picked a safe path between the patches of almost-liquid mud, and they could have crossed the entire former reservoir at its narrowest point if they hadn't been certain that the enemy waited for them on the opposite bank.

Skeeter sat with his legs drawn up under his chin, shivering despite the blanket wrapped around his shoulders. His clothes had dried as he'd walked, the mud flaking away to leave an organic stench of decay that hung around the youth as he sat a few yards from the others.

"You should go back," Reuben said, rummaging in his pack for the last of the travelling biscuits. "We've got little enough food as it is without having to share it with you."

Skeeter shook his head. "Sheriff would blow my brains out soon as he saw me."

"He'd have to find them first."

With a flash of white teeth, Skeeter gave a shy smile. "Can't say nothin' against that. My pa always said I ain't got the brains I was born with."

"Where is your pa?"

"Sheriff hung him."

"Why?"

"We was starvin' and he stole a chicken. It was just him and me, so the sheriff sent me to work on the Miller's farm, and when Josh Miller went to be a deputy, I went with him. Sheriff didn't remember me, I figure."

Asha stirred in the half-light. "Why would you work for the man who killed your pa?"

Skeeter shrugged. "Pa always said to keep your enemies close."

"I don't reckon that's what he meant, exactly," Reuben said, handing half a biscuit to the young man.

"No, I won't eat unless I catch it myself."

"You won't catch much out here," Reuben said, gesturing at the gathering darkness. The clicks and chirrups of birds and insects filled the gaps in their conversation.

"Plenty of eggs. I'll get us some in the mornin'. Look, where you fixin' on headin'? You know Silas and Floyd? They'll be waitin' for us."

Reuben grunted and crunched down on half a biscuit, following it with a swig from his bottle. It was almost empty, and he didn't dare refill it from the stagnant creeks that wound between the little islands. "We don't have a choice. We can't stay out here much longer. Lucifer needs to get back to dry land. But if you can find some eggs in the morning, you can make your own way back. We'll handle our-selves."

"I ain't got nowhere to go back to. Got no family in Flowood and, like I say, the sheriff'll blow my head off as soon as look at me. I'm fixin' to come with you."

Reuben shook his head and gestured at Asha. "I've already got one passenger; I don't need another."

"Please, mister. I can be useful, I promise. I won't drag you down. Let me prove it to you."

"How do you know I'm not as bad as the sheriff?"

"You can't be."

"There's worse than him in the world," Reuben said, touching his wounded arm.

"Besides, you didn't kill him when you could. That's what's making him so mad."

"He's mad that I *didn't* kill him?"

Skeeter nodded. "Sure. He was sore as a skunk when I found him."

"*You* found him?"

"Yeah. He was crying like a baby on account of his leg and bein' afeared of never bein' found. Seemed to me he was drunk, too."

Nodding, Reuben looked into the darkness as if Glass might loom up out of the swamp. "Well, I guess that's why he sent you into the mud. Okay, you can travel with us for now, at least until we can shake off the sheriff."

Skeeter smiled, the relief obvious. "Thanks, you won't regret it, I promise. But where are you headed once we get out of this country?"

Reuben noticed Asha looking up, but he just shook his head. "East. I'm heading east."

He could tell that neither of his companions was satisfied with that answer, but he rolled out his blanket and settled down, and they understood. "Will you take the first watch?" he said to Asha. "Wake me if you see anything."

A chill wind meandered between the islets soothing Reuben's face, though nothing could dull the pain in his arm. As he lay there, he unrolled his potions wrap and found the morphine. He had precious little left and even less prospect of finding any more. And taking one would dull his senses, making him rely on the two youths to keep him safe. But if they were to survive the next day, he had to get a few hours of sleep, and that would only happen if he could ease the pain in his arm.

He swallowed the precious painkiller, and lay on his other arm, trying to keep the wound in contact with nothing but the breeze. How had humanity fallen so far? Thirty-five years after the near extermination of all life on Earth, most people alive today had no access to medication. Over time, painkillers, antibiotics and other essential drugs had become more precious than gold, hoarded by rich organizations and individuals.

Including the Foundation. They preached faith, but used science to treat their own sickness. And mankind had such need of any advantage if it was to survive. He hadn't heard of any census being carried out on a wide enough scale to be conclusive, but he doubted the number of people alive today was any greater than on the first day they'd crawled out of their underground hiding places to find the skies mercifully clear.

Two radiation storms separated by a little over three months had taken the planet's ecology to the brink and they were still at the bottom of the curve. As the drug took effect, Reuben saw images in his mind of the time before the first aurora. He realized with sudden shock that he'd been around Skeeter's age back then and he'd survived through the care of others, though he'd played his part.

And, since then, he'd fallen even farther than his species. Reuben Bane hadn't been his name back then, it was merely a shield to hide behind because he knew, even as he first became involved with the Foundation, that the friends who'd helped him survive the aurora would have been ashamed of his choice.

He shook his head as if denying the truth. But, after all, the aurora hadn't disappeared forever after that second massive storm, and so it had taken many by surprise over the following years. He patted the inside pocket of his jacket where the iridescent patch lay. It was the only way of knowing for sure if the aurora was behind the clouds.

So, there had been the two swift strokes that almost sterilized the planet. And then seemingly endless recurrences that, though much less severe, nevertheless thinned out the surviving populations of people and animals. Few unborn children survived to term in those early years, and those who did were often burdened with deformities and sickness. And so he'd bought into the Foundations dogma, seeking to protect the genome from further pollution. Better a thousand pure humans than a million blemished souls.

And, though he'd been an instrument of that doctrine, he still could hardly believe that he hadn't seen its stupidity. It had taken many years and a woman to begin his journey, then tragedy and the mercy of strangers to set him on his current path.

He breathed in the fetid, organic smell of the old reservoir, yearning to feel solid ground beneath his feet. Together with Skeeter and Asha, he was confident he'd find his way out of this decaying landscape.

Finding his way to redemption, though, that was a whole other story. He couldn't see the road to that, let alone any pathway to forgiveness.

26

NADIA

ZAK WATCHED AS THE girls filed into the chapel. He and Jacob were perched in the roof space beside the windows they'd just finished cleaning.

The swollen figure of Father Ruiz entered first, with Sister Greer walking beside him, and then the girls, led by sisters who were, presumably, their teachers. It was all familiar enough to Zak. He'd spent his entire childhood in an orphanage after his parents died in the last major plague outbreak. All he had of them were some vague memories of events, words and faces he wasn't certain were theirs at all. They could equally have been the faces of his early carers.

Although *carer* wasn't the word he'd use for it. Sure, he was fed — though barely enough — clothed in the shameful uniform of the orphanage and given a form of education. A cruel and limited form. Mr. Hoffman had been the only ray of light in that dark time, and he'd been forced to go to extraordinary lengths to teach selected children. Sometimes, Zak thought he'd have been better off remaining in ignorance, but without Mr. Hoffman, he wouldn't have met Mr. Wong and gotten his job as an under-servant. The two had some kind of arrangement, though Zak hadn't yet worked out the nature of it.

Jacob, on the other hand, hadn't benefited from Mr. Hoffman's influence. He'd just been lucky to be taken on by the Foundation college. Though he probably didn't feel that way once he went to serve Father O'Brien.

The vast majority of male orphanage graduates ended up working in the fields surrounding New Boston or, if they were unlucky, the mines further afield. The unluckiest went to be sailors. Barely more than slaves, they worked the oars of the flat-bottomed wooden vessels that had recently begun to travel along the river channels and hug the new coast of this version of the North American continent.

"Ow!" Zak said, rubbing his arm and turning to look at Jacob.

"You're talking out loud!"

Zak returned his attention to the incoming girls. By all accounts, their lives were no more pleasant than those of the boys — just as filled with cruelty and ignorance, except for the selected few. He looked at the front row of pews. There they were: dressed in white to distinguish them from the light brown uniforms of the other girls, these were the "maidens", selected to be married into the Foundation. He'd never met a maiden face to face, and the orphanage graduates he'd come across among the under-servants all regarded the maidens with jealousy and contempt.

Zak wasn't so sure that was fair. Sure, they got better food, clothes of higher quality and were generally treated more gently than the other girls, but it seemed to him that they were little more than brood mares to the Foundation. But then, he was just a kid himself so perhaps he was missing something.

He didn't understand what criteria the sisters used to select the maidens, but one thing was obvious — they were all beautiful.

Zak settled back to listen to the hymns. It was warm up here and, soon enough, he was dozing until a sharp kick to the ribs woke him again.

He didn't need to look down to know that Father Ruiz was now preaching a sermon. He'd been forced to listen to enough of them to know what its main themes would be. Duty to the Foundation, the subservience of women, the wickedness of the world and how grateful all the children should be for the loving care of the orphanage's sisterhood.

Finally, the father was finished, and Zak watched, transfixed, as the girls made their way out again, led by the sisters, followed by the maidens in their bright whites, long hair tied back beneath compact bonnets. Then the rest of the girls, who shuffled along with less grace. Somehow, Zak found them more fascinating. Less stiff and formal, less adult-like. More like actual people.

He got ready to crawl out of the window and down the outside of the chapel so they could run back to the college, but rather than following the children and sisters out, Father Ruiz settled down into the front pew while Sister Greer came to sit beside him. Zak sighed and his bladder tightened as the prospect of relief receded.

"She is most acceptable," Ruiz said, his voice echoing into the roof space. The fat fool thought he'd checked that everyone had left but hadn't looked up to where Zak and Jacob sat. "And the analysis is confirmed?"

Sister Greer nodded. "Everything is in accordance with scripture."

"And the science?"

"And the science," Greer added with a tone of obvious disdain.

Ruiz emitted a grumbling sort of noise. "The important thing is that they agree. She is, indeed, perfect."

"To be honest, Father, she doesn't seem any different to the other girls."

"But she's perfect scripturally," Ruiz said. "And genetically."

Zak had heard the word genetics before, and now regretted that he hadn't paid enough attention when Mr. Hoffman had mentioned it. It was something to do with what made people look the way they did. Blue eyes or brown eyes. Controlled by tiny things in the man's seed. And it was true of animals and, for all he knew, plants, too.

So, what did being perfect genetically mean?

Then he remembered. His teacher had said that the lights in the sky damaged the seeds and that was what made mutants.

He shook his head. That still didn't answer the question. If mutants had damaged genes and this girl had perfect genes, what did that mean for everyone else?

"And she knows what is expected of her? She will no longer be Nadia?"

Again, the old woman's head nodded. "She knows that much, at least. But of her other ... responsibilities ... at present she believes that she will be the wife of a Father or, perhaps, a Helper."

"As she will. I don't have to tell you it has caused some discord among the brethren. Father O'Brien ..."

The old woman made a disapproving sound. "It is not my place to say, but Nadia's womb must not be wasted on one such as him."

"Please, show restraint!" Ruiz hissed. "The father has much power."

"Then I suggest you arrange the marriage for as soon as possible."

Zak gasped. The girls didn't leave the orphanage until they were sixteen. He'd never heard of a wedding taking place while the girl was still a maiden.

"I'm sure she will please you, and it is good that her first husband will be a gentle man, such as yourself."

Slapping a hand over his mouth, Zak stared, wide-eyed at the two old people below. So, that was what this was all about? That disgusting old man was picking out a bride?

He missed what Ruiz said in response. The old woman was speaking again. "I pray that your seed is quickly fruitful, so you may have longer with her to teach her the way of things."

Ruiz made that grumbling noise. "Yes, it would be my duty to keep her for as long as possible. But one cannot be selfish with so much at stake."

"Indeed, Father. I'm sure Nadia will appreciate your attention."

"Perhaps we should begin referring to her by her new name."

The old woman nodded. "Of course. She will be Eve."

"Here's how it is, boy," Wong said, stabbing the table so hard with his finger that Zak half expected it to get stuck. "You've got to forget it, okay?"

"I don't understand," Zak said.

He and Wong were alone in the kitchen. When they'd gotten back from the girls' orphanage, the chef had silenced them immediately and ordered Jacob to bed before making sure Zak was busy for the rest of the evening.

Now, the building was asleep except for the guards roaming the corridors above, and Wong and Zak. The chef's bulging eyes roamed the kitchen's shadows as they sat together at the table with a single candle between them.

Wong had plied Zak with questions as soon as they were alone. He'd suspected something was happening today — though he didn't explain why — but Zak could tell he was surprised. But there was another, greater puzzle that gnawed at Zak's mind. Why was the chef so interested?

When he'd asked the question, he'd been rebuffed immediately. That was privileged information, Wong had said, Zak's only role was to keep it to himself.

"So, you will tell no one, you understand?"

"Yes, Mr. Wong."

He slammed his fist on the table. If he really wanted to be secretive, Zak thought, he was going the wrong way about it. "You don't talk to me like that."

"Like what?"

"That!"

Zak sighed, sat back and drained the glass of warm milk that had been his only tangible reward for spying on Ruiz. Wong could sometimes be like this and, when Zak had first joined the kitchen staff, he'd found him frightening. But he'd learned that the chef had a kind soul beneath the bluster.

Gazing directly into Zak's eyes, Wong leaned forward. "You have to learn to be better at hiding what you think from others. When you can do this, we talk. But, in the meantime, you will have a new mistress. You must serve her well, and you must be my eyes and ears, even more than before."

"But why do you want to know? I thought you just liked gossip to tell the others."

"You think I enjoy tittle-tattle?"

Zak shrugged, though he wasn't sure what tittle-tattle was exactly.

Wong slammed the table again, but this time more gently. "Well, you are right about that. But I have other reasons. One day, I will tell you."

"When?"

"When I know I can trust you not to blab about me under questioning. I do not want to be put on the fire as others have."

Zak's jaw dropped. "What?"

"Yes, you see it is best you don't know for now. All you have to do is be a good servant to the father and his new wife, and report everything to me, okay?"

"I suppose so," Zak said.

Wong got to his feet. "Good! And one more thing."

"What?"

He bent down until they were eye to eye and wagged a finger at Zak. "One thing you must never do, okay? You hear me?"

"What is it?"

"She is very beautiful, we know. So you must not, absolutely not, fall in love with her, or it'll be you who ends up on the fire."

27

FAWN

REUBEN WOKE UP TO the delicious smell of frying eggs. Without thinking, he raised himself on his elbows, then collapsed in agony as the sleeve of his shirt scraped the wound.

"I told you to wake me," he snapped at Asha, who was crouching beside a small fire.

The boy looked over. "You needed the sleep. And, besides, Skeeter kept watch."

The lanky youth was leaning over the fire poking at a sizzling pan. "I sure hope you don't mind me using this, but I figured we're all pretty hungry and we need an early start. Only got one plate, but you can eat first."

So, he'd survived being at the mercy of Skeeter. Well, that was one way to test whether he could be trusted. He shook his head — he was getting sloppy. Perhaps that was part of his journey. He had to learn to trust. But, more importantly, he had to learn *who* to trust.

Skeeter handed the pewter plate to him. "Didn't have no fat, but they came out fine, I think. Fresh as a daisy, that's for sure. Straight out of the duck's butt."

As if released from a holding spell, a pang of hunger suddenly lanced his stomach, and he took the fork — his fork — and tucked in.

He'd eaten in the halls of the Foundation with the most senior members of the order and had never had a more delicious meal.

As he licked the plate — checking that he wasn't being watched — he handed it back and was about to ask for seconds when he came to his senses. He wasn't an animal, and he knew that respect was the most important element of leadership. And he was, after all, a former exciser.

"I hope I haven't eaten more than my share," he said.

Asha looked hungrily across from his position beside the fire, watching the frying pan. "Skeeter found seven eggs. Three for you, and we get two each."

"You can have one of mine," Skeeter said.

His relief was obvious when Reuben shook his head. "I've already had more than my fair share. Thank you, they were delicious."

He got up and walked over the soggy, grassy knoll to where Lucifer stood. "Sorry, boy," he whispered. "We'll find dry land today, I promise."

He took a handful of grain out of the saddlebag and held it out for the horse to eat, before taking another handful over to where Blossom stood. He knew nothing about the pony's history, but if she'd been the property of the temple, she'd have been fed at least partly on grain and hay as well as grass, and he didn't need either horse to get sick.

And he'd somehow need to find a mount for Skeeter if they were to get far. All his plans — such as they were — had been made with only himself in mind, and now he had to factor in two others.

Neither of his companions was a fighter. Skeeter could presumably handle a rifle, but he didn't have the temperament for violence, if Reuben was any judge. And Asha was just a kid. A kid having to cope with the fact he'd killed a man. How deep was the wound on the boy's psyche, he wondered?

Beyond the little tussock they'd camped on, mist swathed the old reservoir, and Reuben couldn't make out the far bank. And if he couldn't see the bank, then their pursuers wouldn't be able to spot them as they picked their way through the mud.

Skeeter suggested they head north-east rather than straight for the north bank, explaining that this would keep them farthest from the established tracks, taking them deep into the swamps.

After a couple hours of trudging through the mud, Reuben was beginning to regret agreeing to Skeeter's plan. He wanted nothing more than solid ground beneath his feet, even at the expense of a gun battle. After all, the sheriff wouldn't call off the pursuit while they were still in his county, so a gunfight was going to come whether he liked it or not.

They found the river flowing through the bottom of the wide channel it had carved out back when water was plentiful. The West had taken the biggest hit from the environmental chaos caused by the auroras, with deserts extending from the Rockies to the coasts, but the eastern half of the country had suffered in other ways. Here, the Mississippi had shrunken even as the coastal cities had disappeared under rising seas. Most people alive today couldn't remember the rich living green of the Mississippi valley but the evidence was all around them. Like the soggy banks of the Pearl River channel with the shrunken creek running along its bottom.

"What's that land like over there?" Reuben asked.

Skeeter followed his pointing finger. "Them's the swamps."

"Look, we need to find dry ground before we camp tonight. Is that the way?"

"I guess so. I ain't entirely sure. Never been farther. Never been beyond the two towns."

Reuben guided Lucifer up the bank and headed as straight as he could toward a thick wood, the horse's pace picking up as he anticipated the firmer ground.

When they got there, however, the forest floor was littered with the fallen trunks and branches of the trees that had died in the first radiation storms. The wood they were walking through had grown out of the rotting ruin of its ancestors. It was slow progress with Reuben leading the way, holding Lucifer's rein in one hand and his hunting knife in the other.

He didn't have to look behind him to know that the others were following. Asha and Blossom were a few paces back and Skeeter was bringing up the rear, but it was slow going. He found the prospect of camping in these woods little more appealing than the swamp they'd just left. Though they'd be well hidden, they'd get no warning of enemies approaching. Reuben desperately wanted to sleep on a cement floor with four walls around him tonight, but that was looking like a fantasy unless the woods ended soon.

Then he heard the rustle and cracking of feet in the undergrowth.

He froze, raising his hand to stop the others, then search the thickly wooded forest for any sign of movement. Letting Lucifer's reins go, he drew his handgun, sweeping it from left to right as he looked along the sights. It was hard to tell where the sound had come from, deadened as it was by the trees.

Then he saw it, as it first tensed and then relaxed.

"It's a deer," he said, keeping his eyes on the creature as it made its way nervously through the trees. It hadn't seen them, and Reuben's first reaction was to bring the beast down. His stomach churned at the thought of a belly full of venison.

But he couldn't trust the trees to muffle the sound of the shot, and there was no way he'd get close enough to it to use his hunting knife.

Asha drew alongside him, and the deer finally saw them.

"Jeez," Reuben said as the creature regarded them, seeming to know that they were too far away to harm it. "Look at its head."

Asha stood with his jaw open. "It's so beautiful."

The deer's face was separated vertically into two areas, fawn on one side, white on the other. The fawn side sported a small antler, the white side was bare. And, even from this distance, Reuben could see that the eye on the white side was a brilliant scarlet color.

"You gonna shoot it?" Skeeter asked, appearing on the other side of Lucifer. "That's the law. All muteys get the bullet."

If he were still an exciser, Reuben would have dropped the deer already. But then, he'd also have terminated Asha, so he wouldn't have been here to see the mutant animal in the first place. And, in any case, he'd been educated since then and had learned that diversity was everything if the planet was to have a future.

He couldn't help but feel an involuntary revulsion as the creature continued to look in their direction, her head flicking left and right but always returning to meet his eyes. He knew he was responding to his conditioning, but couldn't help gripping his knife.

And then the deer's head snapped to the west, and it was gone. The spell was broken.

"We'd better move," Reuben said. "That could be Glass's men."

They headed toward where the animal had stood, and he found his eyes roaming the forest in case he caught a glimpse of it. Perhaps it wasn't unique. Maybe there was a herd of two-colored deer out here somewhere. Maybe, one day, all the deer in this region would be like it. He shook his head. They wouldn't get the chance. As Skeeter had said, it was the law. Destroy imperfection. Do it yourself if it's an animal.

If it's a human, call the excisers.

28

FOUNDATION

THE MAN FROM THE Foundation looked up at Hannah as she took her seat alongside Ida in the council chamber. His eyes were so dark that it was hard to tell where the pupils stopped and the brown iris began. This, combined with a pallid complexion, lent him a vampiric look that sent chills down her spine. He reminded her of someone she couldn't place. Someone evil.

"The quorum is complete," he said. "You are ..."

"Hannah Myers" she responded. "And *you* are?" She'd be damned if she'd let this creature intimidate her, even if he probably possessed the power to snuff her out at a word.

The man's expression remained fixed as he regarded her. "I am Doctor Carver."

Snider, who was sitting at the head of the council table, said, "Hannah is also a doctor. She's our main scientific advisor."

"Indeed?" Carver said, without moving his eyes from Hannah. "May I ask what your specialism is, or was?"

Hannah puffed out her chest, the effect undermined by her bra creaking. "Astrophysics. Cambridge."

A tiny nod. "Ah, I can see why Mayor Snider chose you. An astrophysicist must be a very useful source of scientific advice."

Being British, Hannah recognized the sarcasm and sent it back the way it had come. "What's *your* doctorate in?"

"Theology."

She scowled. "Oh, very useful, I'm sure."

"I think you'll find it's essential, Doctor. Something of a life skill. Now, why don't we begin the meeting?"

"Are you going to introduce your ... colleague," Hannah said, gesturing at the figure lurking in the shadows of the far corner.

"Of course. Had you been on time, you would know. This is Branch. He will lead any ... research that we carry out in Mecklen."

The man stepped into the light and was revealed to be as different to Carver as she could possibly imagine. He had the scars, wrinkles and deep tan of a man who had spent many years outdoors. He looked to be in his early fifties and so perhaps twenty years older than Carver, and obviously had military experience of some sort though, right now, he was dressed in a perfectly pressed khaki jacket and slacks.

He nodded at her and she returned the acknowledgement without speaking.

"So now that we all know each other, we will begin," Carver said, making a sweeping gesture that encompassed Snider, Hannah, Ida and the other member of the council present, a merchant called Espinoza. Then Carver looked directly at Snider. "With the chair's permission, of course."

Mitchell Snider's eyes rotated toward him and he gave a reluctant nod.

"Thank you. My name is Representative Carver, envoy of the Foundation. I am touring this region to encourage the civic authorities to join our blessed mission so that they may enjoy the benefits of being in communion with our fellowship."

"I'll stop you right there," Hannah said. "We don't wish to be part of the Foundation."

Carver's pale face turned to regard her. "How can you possibly say that when you don't know how your people would benefit?"

"The price will be too high. We know about the burnings in Frederick. We won't submit our citizens to the so-called justice of the Foundation."

The dark eyes had widened momentarily when Hannah mentioned the burnings, but were now as fixed and steady as they had been. "You have been misinformed. Fake news, I might call it."

"Oh, I don't know about that," Ida said, suddenly coming to life. "Seemed pretty darned typical of the Foundation. Promise the Earth, then, when you're let in, you scare folks half to death to keep them under your heel. Well, I'm here to tell you, mister, we ain't gonna have it in Mecklen. We didn't survive all these years with no help from nobody only to hand over our freedom to you."

The old woman, obviously feeling that she'd said all that needed saying sat back and folded her arms.

"And this is the will of the council?" Carver said. "What about you, Mr. Espinosa. The ladies have been quite vocal, what do you have to say?"

Espinoza, a middle-aged man with thinning brown hair and a modest, though high quality, business suit, fidgeted and looked first at Snider before glancing at Hannah. "Representative Carver has traveled a long distance to meet us, and I think we owe him the opportunity to make his case."

Hannah's eyes narrowed as if she were trying to read the truth behind his words. And then she had it. "*You* invited them, didn't you?"

The moment of paralysis was all Hannah needed to confirm her suspicion. "Why?"

Before the merchant could respond, Carver raised his hand. "It is irrelevant. We are here now, and, as Mr. Espinoza says, should we not be allowed the courtesy of making our case?"

Hannah looked across to where Snider sat, as if he'd been frozen in place.

"We will consider that agreed. The most pressing question, I'm sure, is what would Mecklen get out of a closer relationship with the Foundation? Well, we will begin by refilling your grain stores following last year's poor harvest. Your people can look forward to winter with confidence."

Hannah put her hand up. "I have a question."

Carver sighed. "Yes, Doctor?"

"Where does the grain come from? The harvest was poor for most."

"We have sufficient supplies to share with you. It is our sacred duty to ensure that members of the fellowship are fed adequately."

Espinoza nodded. "Let the man speak, Hannah, for heaven's sake."

Hannah subsided, saving Carver's non-answer to her question for later.

"We will also supply much needed security assistance to the civic authorities at a time of increasing tensions across the region. In short, we will provide Mecklen and the surrounding area with a detailed and comprehensive package that will greatly improve living conditions here and offer security for the future. All we need is agreement in principle to move to the next stage."

"And what is that stage?" Snider asked.

Carver gestured at his colleague. "Mr. Branch will instigate an audit of the current situation here."

Snider sat up straight, a puzzled look on his face. "Why is that needed? I can assure you we keep excellent records."

"I'm sure you do, minister. But we're likely to be more ... thorough. And we will investigate the spiritual as well as the temporal. We must be convinced that Mecklen is worthy of our involvement. Pouring grain into a moldy barrel only ruins it all. We must first check that there is no rot."

Snider jumped to his feet. "Now just a damned minute! We will certainly not give you authority to interrogate our citizens!"

"Perhaps you should ask the people, first," Espinoza said. "They want food in their bellies and they want to feel safe from the raiders. I know this because, unlike you, I talk to them every day."

Snider looked at Espinoza with his mouth wide open, his shock impossible to fake.

"It *was* you, wasn't it?" Hannah spat. "You called them in!"

The merchant seemed to shrink in his chair as Ida turned on him.

"You son of a bitch! How many folks have you fooled into thinkin' they'd be better off under the Foundation's heel and feeding off the scraps from their table?"

Espinoza put his hands up, as if fending off a physical attack. "Just let them make their offer! Where's the harm in that? Bowers and Sinclair agree."

So, he'd gone behind their backs and made an alliance with the remaining members of the council. This was starting to feel like an insurrection.

"Exactly," Carver said. He'd been watching the exchange between the councilors with unconcealed delight. "What do you have to lose?"

Hannah sighed. "Everything."

"I'm sorry that you see it that way. However, it's essential for public acceptance that members of the council are treated in the same way as they are. In fact, they must be seen to be exemplary. So, Mr. Branch has Foundation security personnel stationed outside each of your dwellings. By now, they will have searched them and established your status as leading citizens of Mecklen."

Even as Snider roared with anger, sensing the trap closing around all of them, Hannah felt her insides turning to ice.

She ran out onto the dark streets.

"Roberto," she whispered.

Hannah heaved, leaning back against the corner of a building and trying to pull breath into her lungs. She was at the entrance to the checkpoint alley, bitterly regretting that she'd chosen to walk in for the meeting.

"You okay, Minister?"

It was Chester, the old guard holding out a hand so she could straighten up.

"I ... I need to get ... home. Quickly."

Chester rubbed his bearded chin with his free hand, then glanced across at his colleague, a younger man who was pretending not to listen.

"I've an idea, if you're willing."

Hannah nodded — she couldn't speak yet — and followed him to the second house along from the alley.

Outside stood a pony and trap. "You take the cart, Minister, and I'll clear it with the Johnsons. You'll have it back tomorrow, I reckon?"

"Of course. You're sure it's okay?"

"I'll square it with them, you go ahead."

"Thank you," she said, standing on tiptoes to plant a kiss on his hairy cheek, feeling his skin warm instantly.

He helped her into the driver's seat. "Well, I reckon you've got a good reason to be hurrying home," he said, with a wink. "You take care, won't you?"

"Thank you. It's just that I ..." But she couldn't complete the sentence because Chester slapped the pony on the rump, and it trotted on as she fought to steer.

She muttered Roberto's name time and time again, saying prayers to a God she didn't believe in for the kind of miracle that, in her experience, never happened.

Half standing, she strained to penetrate the darkness as she approached the house.

She saw movement, then figures in black and gray fatigues hurried across the road in front of her and disappeared into the night.

Paying no heed to them, she jumped down, then ran as quickly as she could toward the house. The door was wide open, and she felt rage cresting the tsunami of panic as she headed for the room with the trapdoor, ignoring the mess of tumbled documents and drawers in the living room.

The bookshelf had been pushed away and the rug removed, leaving the door itself visible in the gloom. Getting down on her knees, she felt for the handle and heaved it upward, knowing that he couldn't possibly be in here.

And yet she called into the emptiness below, anyway.

"Bobby! Roberto! Are you there?"

But the only sound she heard was the creaking of the house as it cooled, and her own panting as she fumbled with an oil lamp, lit it and shone it into the void.

Nothing.

He was gone.

The only being in this universe that she truly loved was taken by the Foundation.

And tomorrow, they would both burn.

Fists banged on the door.

29

GLASS

REUBEN SET UP HIS camping stove, looking up at the tall, thin figure of Skeeter as the young man watched through a broken window.

An hour before, they'd emerged from the trees into some kind of compound; crumbling buildings scattered around a sequence of rectangular tanks that now sprouted trees. He guessed it had been a water treatment facility or sewage works.

Now, it was a crumbling cement box that, soon enough, would be swallowed up by trees as nature took it back. Already, several weedy saplings lined the inside walls where seeds had landed on soil that had been blown in over the decades.

The sun was close to the horizon, its fading light infusing the room with a green glow. and Reuben hurried to make something for them to eat before darkness came, as they couldn't risk the glow of a fire betraying them once night fell.

The broth he made was poor enough: a mix of dried herbs with cow parsley and bramble leaves they'd gathered from the woods, and a handful of dried salt meat — the last of his supply. It smelled delicious, but he knew it'd ultimately be unsatisfying. They'd all be hungry again soon enough.

"Come and eat," he said to Skeeter. "You ate last this morning, so you'll eat first this evening."

"No need, Mr. Bane, I'm fine. It don't take much to keep me fed," Skeeter said smiling and patting his non-existent belly.

Reuben took the hunting rifle from him and handed over the bowl. "We all need to eat, even you. You're no use to me dead on your feet. And you're having a bath tomorrow, you hear me?"

Skeeter hesitated for a moment, then nodded and moved quickly to sit cross-legged on the floor before devouring the thin broth as if it was a meal fit for a bishop.

Asha, who'd been feeding and tending the horses, hovered to one side, face betraying his hunger.

The boy followed Skeeter and had soon tipped the last of the broth into the bowl for Reuben to eat.

Skeeter resumed his position at the window. It overlooked the main gate, though there were so many gaps in the perimeter wall that their hunters would have to be idiots to come in that way.

Asha had found a high, unbroken window that looked in the opposite direction, and he climbed up before folding himself into place and peering out.

Rummaging in his pack, Reuben found his med kit and set to gently peeling off the bandage he'd applied in haste the previous night. He only had one more clean dressing, so he'd have to find somewhere he could boil some water the following day if he was going to keep the wound from festering.

He winced as he worked, cringing at the smell that rose from the wound. Just as well he couldn't see much, though he had a pretty good idea of how the underside of his forearm looked. It would never fully heal, so the best he could do was to keep it clean and stop it poisoning him while a scar formed. Even if he didn't care much whether he survived for his own sake, he wouldn't allow Keller to win by default from beyond the grave.

He got to his feet and tapped Skeeter on the shoulder. "You get some sleep, I'll take the first watch."

The young man made as if to protest, but exhaustion was obvious in his eyes, so he handed over the rifle and curled up in a corner with a blanket around him, sealing in the stink of dried mud that still clung to him.

"You too," Reuben called over to Asha. "I'll wake you when it's your turn."

Placing the rifle on the windowsill, Reuben began the watch.

Once his companions were asleep, Reuben slipped out to where Lucifer and Blossom were tied up in the remnants of a brick-built shed.

After leaning the rifle against the wall, he ran his hands along Lucifer's flank. He kneeled and took a brush from the saddlebag and ran it down from fetlocks to hooves as the horse stood patiently, working more by feel than by the diffuse moonlight. He'd examine his friend and companion properly in the morning, making sure that nothing unwelcome had lodged where it might fester. He'd run his fingers all over the lower part of Lucifer's legs checking for leeches, but he wouldn't be happy until he could see clearly that he'd gotten rid of everything.

He didn't devote as much time to Blossom: though the mud had come up to her hocks, she was a robust pony who'd probably been exposed to worse over her lifetime. And she wasn't Lucifer. The black horse had been his companion over thousands of miles and a decade and a half. His one constant. He was more of a friend than any human being now alive.

Reuben got to his feet and returned to Lucifer, brushing his back while looking into the darkness. Then he stowed the brush again and picked the rifle up, leaving the shed and making his way slowly around the compound.

As he reached the entrance, looking up and down the road, he jerked back, cursing under his breath as he caught sight of three tethered horses on the other side of the brick wall that surrounded the compound.

Instinctively he looked back to the building where his companions sheltered. At first, he saw nothing, but then there was a flicker of orange light that gathered into the unmistakable glow of flame.

Anger fought with fear as he ran back. He was supposed to be watching! They'd snuck in as he'd groomed the horses and now the night was being ripped apart by fire.

A cry went up, a wailing of terror. Their hunters had shut them in and set it alight. Gasoline, judging by the smell.

Had they bothered to check whether everyone was inside? Did they know he was out here and not in there?

Hope rose in his heart. But he had no time to work out the best tactical approach. He had to free his companions before he tackled the sheriff's men.

Reuben could now see smoke pouring out of the window he'd been watching from. He couldn't head for the door as they'd surely be watching it, and he couldn't remember if there had been another way in. No, he'd have to smash the window.

He hit something hard and staggered, hands slipping down a sapling as a shape lurched out of the shadows, arm swinging.

Instinctively, he ducked beneath the sword blade, then came up under the arm, grabbing the other hand, feeling the warm metal of a pistol that he wrenched away.

The other man fell back, overbalanced by the ferocity of his attack, but then kicked out, winding Reuben and sending him sprawling backward. The figure rushed for him, silhouetted against the flames, sword raised.

But Reuben Bane had been a scrapper since long before his attacker was born and his fingers had already found his Colt. He brought it up and the man fell even as Reuben rolled away to avoid the dropping body.

Bane got to his feet, ignoring the pain in his wrist, back and gut as he surged for the window. He stooped to pick up a fallen brick and hurled it at the pane, shattering it and condemning another fragment of the old world to history.

Climbing onto the brick sill, he brushed off the remains of the glass with his elbow and called into the room.

"Asha! Skeeter!"

He heard nothing, but Asha staggered into view, reaching the window with breath rasping in his throat.

"Where is he?"

The boy shook his head, unable to get any words out.

Reuben grabbed him by the shoulders and lifted him through the window frame. "Go! Lose yourself in the trees. Come back in the morning. You got me?"

"I don't ..."

"No time! I've got to help him. Now, go!!"

And Reuben shoved Asha away before wrapping his coat collar over his mouth and climbing into the inferno.

Over the snap and crackle of the all-consuming flame, Reuben heard gunfire from outside. So, there was at least one more man out there. Asha was fast and small and would make it to the trees in seconds — he had a chance. Which was more than Skeeter did if Reuben didn't find him quickly.

He checked the corner where he'd last seen the young man, but there was no sign of him there. Then he looked over at the shut door and gasped as he spotted Skeeter's body, curled up on the floor.

Reuben ran over and shook the recumbent form, but got no response, so he began dragging him across the floor toward the window. He looked over his shoulder, retching as the oily smoke penetrated his lungs. There was no way he'd get Skeeter out unless he woke, he simply didn't have the strength anymore.

In desperation, he walked over to the door and kicked out with all his strength, feeling the rotten wood give. One more kick and it burst open. Reuben felt the gathering heat on his back, grabbed Skeeter's shoulders and, with a final effort, hauled him across the threshold, before falling on his back among the detritus outside.

"Well, now, ain't that sweet?"

Reuben looked up into the baleful eyes of Sheriff Glass and all hope left him.

"Rescuin' a mutey, then this sack of useless bones. Mighty odd behavior for a exciser. I got two rounds left in this weapon, so you can watch your new friend die before I leave you to bleed out. You know we got wolves in these parts now, don't you? On account of all the deer, I guess. You get them sat up, Floyd, and we'll get vengeance for poor old Silas that this son of a bitch killed in cold blood."

30

EVE

HE FELL IN LOVE with her the first moment he met her.

Father Luiz looked up from his desk as Zak entered and gestured lazily at the girl standing in front of him. "Ah, Isaac. This is Eve. She is to be your new mistress."

Zak almost forgot to look suitably surprised, he was so transfixed by the face that turned to glance at him before looking back to the desk, head downcast.

Fortunately, Mr. Wong had endlessly repeated how important it was that he feigned innocence, and that snapped him out of his hypnotism. Bright blue eyes on a pale, perfect face, framed by yellow hair tied back at the nape of her neck.

"Father? I don't understand," he managed.

Ruiz harrumphed as if Zak was being particularly dense. "You know that I was once married?"

"Yes, Father, you told me. It was before you became a shepherd."

"Indeed," he said, nodding his massive head. "In fact, it was before I joined the Foundation. It was before the angelic lights appeared in the sky to herald the beginning of the end. Martha, my wife, was taken by God during those weeks. It was a sad time, you understand, my boy?"

"Yes, Father."

In an instant, the priest's face transformed into a scowl, and he slammed his hand on the desk surface. "No! How can you possibly know? You did not experience it. Don't be a fool, boy."

"Sorry, Father." Zak wondered how the loss of his parents when he was a young child weighed on the scales of grief in comparison.

Ruiz sighed and leaned back. "I don't know why I bother, but you are part of my household, so you must know."

"Thank you, Father."

"Martha and I were not blessed with a child. And you are aware of Foundation doctrine when it comes to men of the faith? What do we teach?"

At least this was more solid ground. "'The man is to plant his seed so that the faith spreads.' Is that correct, Father?"

Ruiz nodded, muttering a reluctant acknowledgement. "I have failed in that duty, Isaac, and my time grows short. Eve, here, has consented to be my wife and to bear my child."

Zak couldn't help but notice Eve's body tighten as Ruiz said that, but the shepherd was focused too closely on Zak's reaction to notice.

"That is ... good news, Father. I congratulate you both."

Ruiz stood clumsily and held out a hand. For a moment, Zak wasn't sure what to do, but he'd seen Wong do the same with Mr. Hoffman, so he copied his friends and stepped forward, extending his right arm. His hand disappeared into the sweaty mass of Ruiz's paw as the priest squeezed so hard, Zak winced.

"Now, embrace your new mistress," Ruiz said, releasing him.

With obvious reluctance, Eve allowed him to put his arms around her and draw her into a light hug. Her hair smelled of summer flowers, and her white dress was as smooth and blemish-free as her skin. And she was trembling.

"That will do," Ruiz said, smiling as they pulled apart. "You see, Isaac, though she and I are to be married soon, I have other duties. And, at those times, you shall be her protector."

Zak's jaw opened wide. "Father? But ... but I have ..."

"You will carry out your other duties when I am with Eve. I have spoken to Mrs. Pietersen, and the time will be found." Then, he looked at the girl. "My dear, will you wait in my reading room? I have words I must say to Isaac."

They both watched as she shut the door of the small antechamber. Zak knew what he was thinking, but wasn't so sure about Ruiz.

"Now then, Isaac," the priest said. "You can see how precious she is, can't you?"

"Yes, Father."

"She is now your little sister. Not like the sisters of the Foundation, but a blood sister, do you understand?"

In truth, he didn't understand at all, but he nodded anyway.

"And any big brother would wish to protect his little sister, would he not?"

"Of course, Father."

"Good. Because there are people who would harm Eve."

"Father?"

Ruiz smiled, enjoying Zak's obvious surprise. Then his smile vanished and he leaned forward, his face expanding like a puffer-fish as he rested his chins on his chest. "I am about to bring you into my confidence. You know why, Isaac?"

"No, Father."

"It's because I trust you. You have been a faithful servant this past year and deserve this promotion."

Promotion?

"Thank you, Father. But I don't understand why Mistress Eve would be in danger here."

"Of course, my boy, how could you? But be assured that she *is* in danger. What do you know of the maidens?"

Zak composed his thoughts for a moment, sorting between those things he could reasonably know of them and those that he had learned from Wong. "Just that they are intended to marry important members of the Foundation, Father."

"How are they selected, do you think?"

"Well, they're all pretty, Father."

Ruiz's grin returned and he leaned back in his chair, placing his hands across his wide stomach. "That is true, my boy, that is true. But there's more to it than that. Do you know that beauty is one way that our Lord God shows us what is good, just as ugliness is a sign of evil?"

Zak hoped his nodding agreement looked authentic to the priest. Sure, Eve was beautiful, but Ruiz himself certainly wasn't. He'd heard stories of how a princess kissed a frog to turn him into a handsome man, but he wondered whether that worked with toads like the father.

"But there are many other steps that the sisters go through to select maidens. Do you know of the Institute of Science?"

"Not much, Father."

Again, the patronizing nod. "Of course. The Institute spearheads our scientific interpretation of the Holy Bible. They have certain methods that enable us to determine the — how shall I put it? — *goodness* of a maiden or, indeed, anyone. You see, my boy, our task is to prepare for the second coming of our Lord, but he will only return to a world that contains humans fit for his kingdom. The war with Satan thirty-five years ago produced many impurities, even among those who appear normal. So, our holy excisers go among the people and identify those with physical imperfections while we, here, work at the other end of the problem, by bringing about an improvement in the human race. The maidens are our means to do this."

Zak didn't respond immediately; his mind was reeling both from what he was learning and the trust Father Ruiz was showing in him.

"Do you understand what I am saying?"

"Yes, Father. I think so."

Again, he leaned forward and jabbed a flabby finger at Zak. "But you see my boy, Eve is the first maiden to be judged entirely perfect. She is to be the source from which the future of humanity is to be derived. But I am not the only one to know this, and there are others who are jealous, and more who do not agree with our doctrine. So, you must protect her when I cannot."

"But, Father, I'm not a warrior."

He straightened up again. "No, but you will be. Tomorrow, you will begin your training."

Zak nodded enthusiastically. "Yes, Father! Who will it be?" He imagined one of the security guards who roamed the corridors at night.

"His name is Barber."

Shock ran through Zak's frame. He knew that name.

Ruiz grunted, acknowledging the transparent astonishment on Zak's face. "Yes. Tomorrow, you train with the master sergeant. Try not to let him kill you."

31

FLOYD

REUBEN LEANED BACK AGAINST the brick wall and waited for death. He'd suffered more these past couple of days than he'd have imagined he could cope with, and he became curiously relaxed as he sat, looking straight ahead. At least the pain would end soon.

Skeeter had woken as Floyd pulled him upright beside Reuben while Sheriff Glass hobbled restlessly, trying to keep his injured foot off the ground as much as possible.

"Come on Floyd! Let's get this done, then you can go finish off that mutey hidin' in the woods."

Floyd got to his feet and stood beside the sheriff as Skeeter looked up at him.

"F ... Floyd ..."

Glass laughed. "Good, you're awake to see justice done, you filthy traitor. I knew you was a good for nothin' from the moment you begged me to let you join the watch. Thought I didn't recognize you, didn't you?"

Reuben glanced at Skeeter, whose face had tightened in shock and fear.

"Yeah, I remembered hanging your thief of a father. But I took you on anyway."

"Why?" Reuben asked, unable to stop himself.

Glass snorted. "It made me laugh. Spent the past three years makin' his life a misery, so thank you very much for finally tipping him over the edge. I don't reckon he'd ever have found the balls if you hadn't come along. So, you see, this is all your fault."

The sheriff bent down and looked Reuben in the eye. "First it was Wilcox, Bailey and Delacruz, then poor Yates, then Silas and him with a wife and child. Heaven only knows how many others you've killed. You deserve to die a dozen times over. It's just a shame I've only got two rounds in my gun."

He stood up again and rubbed his chin. "Hold on, I know. Floyd, you can have the honor of avenging your friend. Put a bullet in his brain so I can use both rounds on this filth."

"Shouldn't he stand before a judge?" Floyd responded.

"And what will that judge say? They're guilty as hell, and that's where they're bound. No, all that does is put justice back a few days. You don't think they're guilty?"

Floyd grumbled something, then gestured at Reuben. "He sure is. But it's for the judge to say, ain't it?"

"You refusing to do what I order, son?" Glass said. "Don't you forget who I am, will you?"

"No sir, I remember."

"Your momma and I have an arrangement, don't we?"

"Yes, sir."

"But she lives out on that farm when it'd be better for her to come into town. If her son don't follow orders then I don't reckon she'll be safe out there. Maybe she'll have to take me up on my offer. You want that, boy?"

"No, sir."

Reuben saw the revulsion on the younger man's face. He was a little older than Skeeter, though that might simply be because his beard gave him a mature appearance. Reuben dismissed the random thought and looked back up at the sheriff.

"Then shoot that goddam traitor," Glass said, jabbing a finger in Skeeter's direction.

Floyd raised his weapon, but hesitated long enough for Glass to grab it. "I'll do it myself, then, but your momma's gonna hear about it, and she's gonna wish you did as I said. She sure is gonna pay,"

Glass pointed the weapon — a modern cap and ball revolver — at Skeeter, who'd gone rigid and screwed up his eyes.

Suddenly, Reuben kicked out, catching Glass's wounded leg and send the sheriff into a howling rage, spinning around with the revolver in one hand and his rifle in the other.

Then, as the sheriff brought himself back under control, he pushed Floyd away and brought the revolver down, pressing it against Skeeter's forehead, and hissed, cheeks purple with rage. "Now die, you worthless son of a —"

Then he groaned, and collapsed sideways, a knife protruding from his side.

Floyd fell to his knees. "I'm real sorry, Sheriff."

"You ..." Glass grimaced as pain lanced his side. "Why?"

"Skeeter's my buddy. And you ain't gonna hurt my momma."

Reuben grabbed Skeeter's arm and helped him to his feet, the two of them looking down at the sheriff, who was groaning as the filthy concrete beneath him turned dark.

Leaning over him, Floyd began rocking back and forth, moaning, "What have I done? I'll hang for this, sure for certain I will. I ain't killed no one before."

"But you were sent to hunt us down," Reuben said.

"Silas was in charge. He's killed. Not me."

Reuben put his hand on Floyd's back as the sheriff finally went still. "Give me the knife," he said.

Looking up, Floyd then glanced across at Skeeter, who nodded, then, with a grunt, he pulled the knife out of the sheriff's body.

"Here," Reuben said, drawing his own knife from its scabbard at his belt. "Coat this in blood and take it back with you."

Floyd turned the blade over in his hands. "This an exciser's knife?"

"Tell folks you arrived too late to help the sheriff and Silas, but chased us off after I'd killed him, then you took the blade. I don't reckon you'll get any awkward questions as long as you get your story straight as to why you were separated from them first. In fact," he said, reaching down and picking up the revolver. Without warning, he shot Floyd, and the young man dropped.

"What the hell?" Skeeter cried out. "He saved my life! He weren't gonna kill you!"

"And I haven't killed him," Reuben said, nudging the man's body with his toe. "But that flesh wound to his arm will make his tale all the more believable. Now, we've got to find the boy and get on our way."

Reuben watched Floyd ride away, leading Sheriff Glass's horse toward Flowood.

"He'll make it, you think?" Skeeter said, petting the face of Silas's former mount, a bay gelding.

Reuben nodded. "Should do. As long as he gets his story straight." They'd used a strip torn from Silas's shirt to bind up Floyd's arm, doing it effectively but also untidily, so it would seem he'd treated himself. The round had nicked the flesh at the back of his arm and looked a lot worse than it was.

Floyd was going to take his time to return to the temple before raising the alarm. That would give Reuben, Skeeter and Asha the chance to get away before any hunt was up. Reuben thought it unlikely that whoever took over as sheriff would rush to gather another posse, but it paid to be careful. Most lawmen preferred to keep out of exciser matters and they'd have enough trouble dealing with the two Foundation men who'd died in their townlands without risking further casualties chasing down a lost cause.

But he'd learned not to trust in the sense and rationality of men, so they were going to get out of Madison County as quickly as they could.

At least they'd found Asha quickly. He'd been lurking in the trees and responded immediately when Reuben called. The boy was physically none the worse for wear except that he stank of burned hair and had lost his eyebrows. Physically okay, but mentally, who could say?

Blossom and Lucifer waited patiently with the remaining horse while Reuben packed his saddlebag with the provisions they'd taken from Glass, Silas and Floyd. He handed the cap and ball revolver Silas had carried to Skeeter. It was a modern model based on a US Navy pistol of the mid-nineteenth century and seemed unusually well made. He'd bet good money Silas hadn't bought it originally — a quality weapon like this would have been out of the reach of any ordinary man.

"You okay?" he said as he glanced over at Skeeter who was rubbing at the back of his head.

"Yeah. Sheriff knocked me out before he locked us in. I'll be okay."

"Just as well he didn't take the time to check whether I was in there with you."

Skeeter nodded. "I think he was afeared of you."

"You stink of gasoline."

"Yeah. And swamp mud."

"We all need to clean up, but for now we've got to get away. You know you've got to come with us? You can't come back here even now if you wanted to."

Skeeter turned toward Reuben, his normally open face now almost comically serious. "I know. If I went back, they'd hang Floyd. He's a good fella underneath all the BS. Maybe he'll make sheriff someday."

Climbing into Lucifer's saddle, Reuben watched as Skeeter nudged his bay alongside. Asha appeared on the other side, looking up from Blossom's back.

"So, where are we headed?" he asked.

Reuben gazed into the distance. "East," he said. "First to find somewhere we can rest up a little and get clean and healed."

"What then, boss?" Skeeter said.

"Then I complete my task."

"We'll help, won't we Ash?"

"Yeah," the boy said enthusiastically. "If you let us."

Reuben shook his head, as if giving in to the inevitable. "Sure. I haven't been able to shake you off so far."

"So, what's this task?" Skeeter asked as they trotted forward together.

"I need to find a woman."

Skeeter laughed out loud. "Don't we all? Sorry, boss."

"This is one particular woman. I'll tell you her story one day, or as much as I know. She headed east a long time ago and I don't even know if she's alive, but the folks who sent me want her back or, at least, to know she's dead."

"Why is she so important?" Asha asked.

Reuben shook his head. "I don't know, for certain. Only that she has vital knowledge."

"And who are these folks who sent you? I mean, who sends an exciser?"

"Former exciser," Reuben said. "As for who sent me, they come from a place called New Haven."

EPILOGUE

GENERAL RUSSELL REID STOOD on the lip of the valley, breathing in the salt tang as his binoculars swept over what had been Downtown Seattle.

"Well, Mackey? What news do you have for me?"

The footsteps from behind froze, and he smiled grimly to himself. Did the idiot think he could sneak up on a former SEAL? General Reid wasn't quite that old, or that deaf. When the likes of Doctor Mackey could get the better of him, then he would gladly hang up his service revolver and jump into the bay. In the meantime, he had his mission.

The scientist moved into his peripheral vision as Reid continued to look out over what had been West Bay and the industrial district, but was now open water. "Sergeant Guthrie reports they are on their way back, General."

"Good. Status?"

"Success. No casualties."

"Collateral damage?"

Pause.

"Perhaps it would be best to ask the sergeant, sir."

Reid grunted. Perhaps, indeed.

"I will go down and meet them," the general said as his binoculars found the RIB powering toward the shore. "I expect a full report within twelve hours."

He spun around, ignoring the spasm of annoyance on the big, bearded face of the scientist, and strode toward the path down to the shoreline. Mackey was useful to him, if only because without him, Reid would have to deal with the other scientists himself, and Reid always came away with a sour taste in his mouth when he had to do that. It was one thing to choose to sacrifice conscience for the greater good of humanity, but it was quite another to completely disregard it in pursuit of scientific advance. Not all progress was good, and Reid's role, as he saw it, was to direct the energy of the eggheads toward his goals rather than letting them head off down infinite rabbit-holes guided only by their individual curiosity. He looked forward to a time when he no longer needed them.

Sergeant Guthrie was striding through the water toward the shore as Reid approached and managed to snap a salute as he saw the general.

"Report, Sergeant."

Guthrie straightened, then followed Reid as he walked along the bank toward what had once been the local library building, now half submerged and rotting.

"All mission objectives achieved, sir."

"Casualties?"

"None, though X-16 sustained a minor serration to his arm."

Reid looked over to where the soldiers were wading through the gently lapping waves, guns and packs on their shoulders, carrying fragments of old technology they'd taken from the tower. The arm of one was naked save for a blood-soaked bandage.

"How did it happen?"

"A woman darted at him with a knife, and he hesitated, just for a moment."

Reid followed the movement of the injured soldier as he reached the bank. "Be sure to report this to the geek squad. A pity. In every other respect he scores in the upper nineties. What is it, sergeant?"

"Permission to speak off the record and candidly, sir."

"Granted."

Guthrie, a late middle-aged career NCO, had joined the forces at roughly the same time as Reid, just before the fall. The general trusted this man more than just about anyone else, which made him both useful and dangerous.

"Well, it's just that X-16 is the best of them, sir. It'd be a shame if we lost him."

The soldiers were now out of view, so Reid broke protocol by slapping the sergeant on the shoulder. "I know what you mean, George, but that just shows his weakness. What was it like over there?"

"Honestly, sir, it was a horror show. Now, you know me, I'm a hundred percent on board, a hundred percent loyal."

You'd better be, Reid thought.

"Yes, George. Go on."

Guthrie glanced up the slope, as if to check they were alone. "But I'm not going to pretend it's easy to see them in action. The defenders didn't stand a chance."

"I understand, but that's the entire point, isn't it?"

"Yes, sir. Of course. But it's, I don't know, creepy seeing them. Like a bunch of terminators."

"Except X-16?"

"X-16 performed perfectly except for that momentary hesitation."

"Which almost got him killed."

Guthrie nodded. "Yes sir."

"You understand, George, that they have to be efficient because, they will only be few, at least until the breeding program bears fruit."

"Yes, sir."

"It's a pity that X-16's offspring will no longer qualify for the elite units, but perhaps we can find a role for them in support."

Guthrie nodded.

Reid put his hand on Guthrie's upper arm. "Be strong, George. I understand the toll this is taking on you, but the squad will need babysitting for a while yet. If Mackey is right, he'll soon be able to identify a candidate to replace you as leader, and then you can enjoy a well deserved retirement."

"I'll be honest, sir, I'm looking forward to that day."

"As am I. Now, make sure the salvaged equipment is delivered to Mackey and grab yourself some food and sleep."

Guthrie snapped to attention again, then spun on his heels and headed quickly up the muddy slope.

Reid remained there as a couple of regulars pulled the RIB onto shore and fastened it to the exposed iron frame of an unidentifiable building. They'd stayed away until the squad had disappeared, and he couldn't say he blamed them. He'd heard that the regular soldiers referred to their elite brethren as the Terminator Squad and, frankly, he approved, though he stuck to the official designation of Shark. Either worked.

The experiments had been ongoing even when he'd joined the Army forty years before. He'd had the good fortune to be assigned to the staff of General Agnew of the Army's battlefield research division. At a time when most of the energy and attention was being focused on semi-autonomous weapons like drones and artillery pieces, Agnew had hived off a little of the budget to focus on the "wetware" — the human factor. To him, the technological arms race would end in the destruction of the species unless people remained in control, and for that to be the case, the human component would also have to improve, keeping pace with the machines.

So, he'd instituted the Achilles program, looking into the genetics of the perfect soldier. He was hamstrung by the fact that, even if he could identify the blueprint, he couldn't institute a breeding program to produce soldiers with those traits. Ethics and all that.

Since the fall, however, this hadn't been a concern. The first thing Reid had done as he worked his way up the thinned out post-fall Army hierarchy, was to search for the weapons Agnew had control of. Agnew himself had died in the first wave, and Reid had thought the secret of his cache had gone with him, but then, by a stroke of luck, the general had discovered a clue to its location. The materials returning from the tower would hopefully yield it up.

Reid nodded to one of the regulars as he strode up the beach. Soon enough, he would have control of a forgotten but deadly technology, and the soldiers to make the most of it. He chuckled to himself as he thought of Guthrie. A good soldier, hampered by only one thing. A conscience.

Agnew had told Reid that building the perfect soldier was about more than adding attributes — strength, agility, the urge to follow orders — it was also about removing those that were inconvenient. It had taken only two generations for Reid to manage it and he smiled as he strode back to the base to supervise Mackey's search. Soon, he would have a cache of unbeatable technology and the perfect squad to supplement it. And then, just watch him. He would remake America in his image. Neither the Republic of Texas nor the feeble Federal government would stand in his way. The Foundation was his true opponent, and he knew they were tinkering with selective breeding at their headquarters on the East Coast. But they were looking the wrong way down the telescope, pursuing a mythical, unachievable perfection. Human beings entirely devoid of any mutations. A pure genome to breed from.

Reid had no such aims. To him, the survivors were mindless sheep crying out for the rule of order, and he was the man to bring it. And he wouldn't pervert his religion to do it. He would simply be the instrument, as Moses had been.

And sometimes it was necessary to use tools of great power and destruction, even with regret. Sometimes it was necessary to discover what it was that stood in the way of soldiers carrying out their orders to perfection, and to remove it.

Agnew had known, but Reid was the one to actually do it.

He'd removed empathy. He'd created a squad of psychopaths with an addition to prescription drugs. They would sweep away all opposition before they, themselves, would be eliminated, their task complete. One final sleeping tablet.

Reid walked along the clifftop toward the base, glancing out over the sea at the rotting towers beyond. Suddenly, he shivered. Was it the fresh breeze? Or was that an unfamiliar and forgotten emotion? Was it fear?

That night, by the light of a gently flickering incandescent bulb, he picked up the book. The gold lettering of the title had faded completely, but the name of the author was still visible. Mary Shelley.

AUTHOR'S NOTE

I hope you enjoyed the first Reuben Bane book. As you now know, it's set thirty-five years after the apocalyptic events featured in the Nightfall series. There's no need to have read that series to enjoy this one, as it only forms the background for these books. In this book, we meet at least one character from the previous series, though much has changed after three and a half decades.

One of the themes of my books is the triumph of flawed but essentially good human beings over the challenges they face. With post-apocalyptic fiction, the chief antagonist is often the event that causes the end of the world, which is generally (in my writing) a natural event of one sort or another. But it seems inevitable to me that while this would bring the best out of some people, it would bring the worst out of others. So, my characters spend as much time battling against the evil intentions of their fellow humans as they do contending with the indifference of the natural world.

This is dialed up a notch in these latest books. The world has settled down into a new, though harsh, normal. Nature continues to make it hard for humanity to recover even as the climate rocks back and forth. But the principal challenges come from the people and organizations that oppose rebuilding a society that can thrive for the benefit of all.

So, we have the Foundation, a cult-like religious organization that is inspired by — though not based on — several real-life groups. They survived the apocalypse because they were better prepared, and their doctrine requires that they, in turn, now look forward to the event their prophecies predicted, even at the cost of the people living such difficult lives.

How would they use the situation to their advantage? By this point, most people alive at the time had been born since the apocalypse and therefore have no memories of the world we inhabit today. Technologically, humanity has been propelled back to, at best, the Victorian age, with agriculture falling further behind. A medieval peasant would feel right at home in the fields around Mecklen, Jackson or New Boston.

The next books will expand upon this, but they also focus on the inner struggles of our main characters as they fight to stay true to themselves and, in Reuben's case, to atone for a dark past in which he was, himself, a part of the organization he now opposes.

I hope you'll come along for the ride.